"A loving send-up of the stereotype of the prim librarian."
The New York Times

"Exciting…Appealing…Miss Zukas is straight-forward, understated, tongue-in-cheek."
The Armchair Detective

"You're in for a good time."
Toronto Sun

"An enchanting series. I love Miss Zukas mysteries."
Carolyn Hart

"Dereske has a sharp eye for the subtleties of small-town life."
Seattle Times

"Recommended."
Montgomery Advertiser

"The mild mannered Miss Zukas proves her mettle battling the elements in several super action scenes, not to mention battling wits with a cold-blooded murderer."
Alfred Hitchcock Mystery Magazine.

FAREWELL, MISS ZUKAS

Jo Dereske

June Creek Books

This is a work of fiction. All characters in this book are fictitious, and any resemblance to actual persons, living or dead, is purely coincidental.

June Creek Books
P.O. Box 627
Lynden, WA 98264

Copyright © 2011 by Jo Dereske
ISBN: 0983374503
ISBN-13: 9780983374503
Library of Congress Control Number: 2011923024
www.jodereske.com

For Jurgita Rudzioniene
and
Danute Karliene

CONTENTS

CHAPTER 1

A Night to Remember

Late on Saturday night, after an evening during which she had finally made up her mind for good and for real and for true—no room for take-backs—Miss Wilhelmina Cecelia Zukas retired to her bed in exhaustion so complete she neglected to brush her teeth, neglected to remove her slipper socks, and for the first time in the twenty years she'd lived in the Bayside Arms, she forgot to lock her door.

She may not have shifted a muscle all night long, since when she awoke, she discovered herself to be in exactly the same position she recalled being in when she'd fallen into troubled slumber: lying on her back, legs slightly parted, her hands loosely folded over her stomach.

What had finally roused Helma was a screeching wail, a sound she initially believed to be the sirens of approaching emergency vehicles.

Danger, danger.

She sat bolt upright in bed without the aid of her hands, blinking and taking stock of her surroundings, already throwing back her covers to flee to safety.

The wail repeated itself, definitely as insistent as an ambulance siren, but now she recognized the irritated yowling of Boy Cat Zukas. Helma relaxed and glanced at her clock radio. It read 1:18.

1:18?

Light filtered between her closed bedroom curtains. She discerned distant voices, cars passing on the street outside the Bayside Arms. The evidence was irrefutable. It was 1:18 on Sunday afternoon, not the lingering middle of Saturday night.

Fourteen hours? She'd been asleep for *fourteen* hours? Helma's eyes were sticky, her mouth as dry as dust, and she was desperate to use the bathroom. She completed pulling back the covers and swung her legs over the side of her queen-sized bed.

And saw her slipper socks.

And remembered.

"Oh, Faulkner," she breathed, and dropped back onto her pillow, reaching for the beribboned edges of her blankets and pulling them to her chin.

Boy Cat Zukas, as if aware she was conscious and therefore needlessly forcing him to wait, emitted a volley of meows, this time accompanied by the scritch-scratch of cat claws on the sliding glass doors to her balcony.

Helma closed her eyes, inhaled to the count of four, held her breath for four, then exhaled to the count of eight. Again. Then again.

That did it. Swiftly, with her customary economy of motion, Helma swept back her covers into a neat triangle and rose from her bed, ignoring the presence of her slipper socks and reaching for her robe, which every evening she positioned perpendicularly across the end of her bed in case of fire, emergency phone calls, or unexpected pounding on her apartment door.

Her robe wasn't there. With a slight shrug of irritation, she retrieved it from her closet and carried it with her as she hurried to her bathroom, where, risking more cat scratches on her glass door, she also brushed her teeth, keeping her eyes firmly averted from the mirror.

In her living room, Boy Cat Zukas stood on his hind legs, belly pressed against the glass door and front legs stretched upward. At the sight of Helma, he dropped to all fours and hissed, his goldy-green eyes confronting her with the same suspicion as when he watched her pull her vacuum cleaner from the back of her coat closet.

The former black alley cat didn't curl around her legs or even approach her, nor did Helma reach down to administer a friendly pat on his head. They'd never touched, and that suited both of them just fine. Their relationship was built on a modicum of mutual respect and an abundance of mutual wariness.

Because of the mysterious years he'd spent on his own before he and Helma had formed their reluctant alliance, he possessed: a crooked tail that appeared to have once been broken, bare patches of skin that had grown in white, and a torn left ear—not to mention a diet that resisted her efforts to redirect from small living things to nutritious meals that came in pouches, cans, and boxes.

Before she'd adequately opened the sliding glass door, Boy Cat Zukas squeezed through, pausing to give Helma one last glower before leaping onto the balcony railing, and from there to the roof of the Bayside Arms, and disappearing to do whatever unrepentant alley cats did for feline pleasure. He'd reappear in the evening, just as insistent to enter her apartment as he'd been to escape it. And he'd be either famished or suspiciously round-bellied.

A surprisingly gentle breeze for May slipped into Helma's apartment, the day fleetingly warm and clear. Voices rose from Boardwalk Park beneath her, and to the west, across Washington Bay, the islands piled blue, one on top of the next to the misty horizon. Behind Bellehaven, to the east, on such a clear day Mount Baker would be looming, still white in its brilliant winter coat of snow and glaciers.

After inhaling two deep breaths of the fragrant air, Helma loosened the tie on her robe and re-closed the sliding glass door, pushing down the lock with her thumb and reinserting the wooden safety stick in the door track.

A walk would help clear her mind. Before she had time to return to her bedroom, and while mentally sorting through her closet for appropriately light clothing—beige cotton slacks and a pale blue shirt perhaps—her doorbell rang.

Helma winced, standing stone still. Maybe if she waited it out... But no, the doorbell shrilled like a stuck car alarm. She had no doubt who stood on her doormat. She retied her robe and wearily opened the door without first peering through the security peephole.

She was correct, of course. Ruth Winthrop stood on the third-floor landing of the Bayside Arms, tapping Sunday's rolled and rubberbanded *Bellehaven Daily News* against her palm.

"So what's going on?" Ruth asked, waving the newspaper toward Helma. She wore clashing blue: red-blue capris that on her six-foot frame were nearly shorts, and a greenish-blue shirt that read "Peck & Lambert Paints" on the pocket.

"You're smearing newspaper ink on your hands," Helma pointed out, extending her hand for the Sunday paper.

Ruth glanced down. "Nah, it's paint," she said, relinquishing the paper. "Here, this rag gets skinnier every day, don't you think?"

"Newspapers everywhere are struggling to maintain readership," Helma explained. "With the competition from internet and television..."

"Yeah, yeah. So write an editorial and see if anybody cares." Ruth strode inside past Helma, directly to the refrigerator.

"I'm in need of a diversion," Ruth said from behind the open refrigerator door. "So I call you. For hours I call you. Ring, ring. Nobody answers. She's out on one of her marches up and down our fair city's streets, I think. Or spending her Sunday misguidedly aligning all the book spines in the library. I stop by just to check, you know, in case you've mortally injured yourself dusting your ceiling or shining your stove knobs. And look at you."

"What?"

Ruth emerged from the refrigerator, holding a plastic bottle of orange juice. "It's two o'clock in the afternoon and you're wandering around in your bathrobe. Your hair's all fuzzy. "

"What type of diversion were you looking for?" Helma asked.

"The usual." Ruth waved the orange juice bottle toward Helma's living room. "Let's sit down and discuss."

Helma Zukas and Ruth Winthrop had maintained a bewildering friendship since a rocky beginning in Scoop River, Michigan, when they were nine years old. Having heard harrowing but unfortunately exaggerated tales of the discipline practices of nuns, Ruth's desperate parents had enrolled her in St. Alphonse Elementary School, where the Sisters of St. Casimir had tried their best.

"Teaching Ruth is a daunting task," Helma had overheard Sister Mary Eulogia say to Sister Mary Paulissa in the hallway one day as she was exiting the girls' restroom. "Not daunting," Sister Paulissa had replied with a heartfelt sigh, "Dantean."

Helma chose the rocker in her living room, and Ruth sank into the sofa, balancing the orange juice and a glass in one hand. "I'm going crazy trying to pop some zing into this new batch of paintings. Red is not always a visual solution, forget what the critics say. This whole batch just lies there, dead to the world." She paused, "Kinda like my life. It's about as exciting as buttered noodles."

Helma, who frequently prepared buttered noodles during unsettling times—"comfort food," her mother called the dish— had been reminded too often lately that Ruth was between men, and that lack tended to drain the "zing" from all corners of Ruth's life, including and especially, her art.

"But enough about me," Ruth said, uncharacteristically redirecting the subject from herself. She poured juice into her glass, splashing it on the coffee table and wiping up the spill with the elbow sleeve of her shirt. "So tell me. I know you, Helma Zukas. Sleeping-in is a sign of serious malcontent. Somebody stole the sixteenth volume of the *Encyclopedia Britannica*?"

"The *Encyclopedia Britannica's* online now," Helma told her.

"Of course it is," Ruth said as she absently shoved aside Helma's magazines, which were fanned on her coffee table in alphabetical order by title. "Who wants to look up anything in paper, anyway? They'd have to learn the alphabet."

What was the use? Ruth would find out soon enough. She may as well be first. Helma took a fortifying breath and said it aloud. "He asked me."

"Yet one more time?" Ruth shook her head. "And you said no again. You gotta love the man for his persistence. I can't believe how masochistic he is to—"

"I said yes."

"—punish himself like ..." Ruth's voice trailed off. Her mouth gaped. Her glass slipped from her hand but fortunately it was empty so it rolled harmlessly across the coffee table and came to rest against the juice bottle. "Say that again. I want to see your lips move."

"I said yes."

Ruth whooped and jumped up from the sofa with such vigor that Helma imagined the Henderson's—who lived beneath her—gazing up at their ceiling in alarm. Ruth reached down and gripped Helma's shoulders, lifting her completely out of the rocker. Helma's teeth jarred. "I cannot believe it: You said yes. Oh my god. Stars and stripes forever, hot dogs and weenies. Chicken balls. Did he fall off his chair in surprise?"

"Of course not," Helma said, recalling the expression on Chief of Police Wayne Gallant's face, the way he'd pushed back his chair and clasped both of Helma's hands in his own big, warm hands. How he'd gazed into her eyes as if waiting for the "buts," "excepts," or "laters," his face so pink she'd suspected he was holding his breath

"I cannot believe it," Ruth repeated. "Mrs. Chief of Police. Are you sure 'yes' is the word you used? Look into my eyes and repeat it."

Helma did. "Yes. I said yes."

Ruth abruptly let go of Helma's shoulders and she reached behind her for the rocker to keep from falling. "When's the date?"

"We don't have one. Next summer, probably."

Ruth dropped on the arm of Helma's sofa, frowning, her eyes going distant. "That gives us time to plan. I'll help. We have to think of a theme. You know, like a prom. And colors. Bright ones. I'll paint something, something for your living room. Where are you going to live?"

Helma felt a touch of dizziness, and recalled the covers still open on her bed, still folded open to an inviting triangle. To sleep, she thought idly, perchance to...

"What did your mother say?" Ruth asked, bringing Helma back with a crash. "This has been her fantasy since the time he arrested you."

"He never arrested me, and I haven't told her yet."

"I'm the first?" Ruth clutched her chest in feigned humility. "I'm honored. Well, when she knows, the world will know, so hold on tight."

Helma thought of her mother's reaction and couldn't help it; she stifled a yawn. Maybe just a short nap...

"I'll tell her in a day or so."

"Well, your secret's safe with me." Ruth's voice dropped and her eyes grew misty. "Really, Helm, this is the very best news." She paused, looking somewhere into the middle distance, and

Helma felt a sudden niggling of apprehension. "We're going to have so much fun."

"Ruth," she began cautiously. "It'll be a simple..."

And before she could deter Ruth's musings any further, her telephone rang.

"Go ahead," Ruth encouraged, waving toward the phone on Helma's kitchen counter. "It's probably the man himself, double-checking to see if you've changed your mind."

Helma reached for the phone, reminding herself it might *not* be Wayne Gallant. She'd been in his company only fourteen hours earlier, after all.

"Hello?" She discovered herself to be helplessly expectant.

"Oh, Helma. I can't believe it. I'm so shocked."

Helma's mother's voice sounded undeniably upset, pained. How had the news reached her so quickly? Certainly the chief of police wouldn't have told anyone. Would he?

"Mother," she began, forming words of apology in her mind. "I was planning to call you as soon as - "

But her mother raced on over her, her voice breathless and high with emotion. "Robbery. It was robbery."

"But I *would* have told you first." Helma turned her back to Ruth who was blatantly listening, leaning forward, her expression avid.

"No, no," her mother said. "We were robbed. Em and me. Right here. Right *now*. Robbery."

"Robbery?" Helma repeated. "Hang up immediately and dial 9-1-1."

"I already did that. We're waiting for them." Lillian's breaths exploded against Helma's ear. Hyperventilating.

"Sit down, Mother. Take a deep breath."

"That won't change anything. We were *robbed*."

"A robbery in your apartment? In daylight, while you were there? Are you and Aunt Em all right?"

"Em was here alone. She's...well, she's fine. Almost."

"How did they get inside? What did they take?"

"Not them, he. I suppose he just walked in, but he went out through the window, trying to steal our new television set. Can you believe it? I only bought it three months ago."

"He went *out* the window, Mother? Are you sure that's what Aunt Em said? You live on the fourth floor."

"I know where we live." She said indignantly and dropped her voice. "Em pushed him out the window. He's outside."

Helma felt her heart drop. "Outside? From the fourth floor?" She tried to picture what lay beneath the window in her mother and Aunt Em's apartment: a parking lot. Paved.

"Is he...dead?"

Ruth circled the table to face Helma, her hands and mouth elastic with pantomime. Helma waved her away.

"I can't tell if he's dead from up here. The TV's on top of him. Oh, here come the police. I have to go now. Goodbye dear."

CHAPTER 2

Rear Window

"This is a one-way alley, Helma, and you're not going in the direction our city fathers decreed."

"It's a shortcut to the Silver Gables." On the main streets, sirens warbled and shrieked. Between the buildings, she spotted gyrating red and blue lights, all racing in the direction of the Silver Gables retirement apartments. "We'll avoid the police cordons by taking this route."

She twisted the steering wheel hard, egressing from one alley onto a smaller track that led between the rear wall of a defunct grocery store that had ill-advisedly tried to compete with Hugie's, and a row of Bellehaven's infamous crumbling and mossy one-car garages. A car without tires as highly-rated and well-cared for as Helma's tires might have slewed on the sharp maneuver, but her Buick made the turn as solidly as a high-performance race car. Ruth made a squeaking sound in her throat, anyway.

In her hurry to dress, Helma had grabbed pants and shirt in conflicting blues, so now she resembled Ruth's clashing colors. Her hair was barely combed, and she'd slipped her feet into brown loafers instead of black.

Ruth exhaled in a rush. "Tell me again. Your ancient Aunt Em killed a robber? Dead? You're going to hit that garbage can."

"I see it. *Something's* happened. But Aunt Em is eighty-nine years old. She can't even climb stairs anymore." She swerved around the garbage can and glanced once more toward the emergency lights she'd seen on Cromwell. The tight quarters blocked her view. "I believe there may have been a robbery, but my mother can be very excitable. The story's less dramatic than she claims. I'm sure it is."

Ruth grunted. "Whatever you say. But that juicy bit about the TV sitting on top of a body in the parking lot sounds a little too detailed to be fabricated." Ruth's head swiveled from side to side, her hands moving and pointing at objects Helma was perfectly aware of.

"She said Aunt Em was alone during the robbery." Helma paused, reluctant to admit it aloud, as if saying it would make it even more true. "Aunt Em's grown more ... tenuous this past year."

"Gaga, you mean," Ruth said. "I love her like my own, but face it: Life's growing fuzzy around her edges."

"Occasionally," Helma conceded, "but the facts may still be different than my mother believes."

"Keep trying to convince yourself; I believe her." Ruth braced her hand on the dashboard. "Okay. Slow down. We're here. Both feet hard on the brakes, please."

A uniformed policeman—heavier than most Bellehaven policemen—stepped around the side of the Silver Gables building as Helma pulled her Buick into a Staff Only parking space between the garbage bins and the loading dock. The policeman scrutinized their arrival, holding one hand over the gun holster on his hip. Another policeman followed behind, unreeling a ribbon of bright yellow tape that read, POLICE—DO NOT CROSS.

The heavy officer—who moved more swiftly than she had expected—reached her door as she opened it. "I'm sorry, ma'am. You need to leave this area." He pushed back the brim of his cap with his thumb.

"You may work around my vehicle," Helma told him, removing the ignition key from the Buick that had been her high school graduation present over twenty years earlier, "but please be careful. And lock your door, Ruth," she added.

"This is a crime scene, ma'am." The policeman didn't move from the side of her door. His round pink cheeks gave him a jolly visage at odds with his steely tone of voice.

"That's why I'm here," she informed him politely, pointedly opening her door so it just perceptibly brushed the pants of his uniform, though certainly not touching his body. "Now if you'll excuse me."

He opened his mouth, but Ruth, who'd already leapt from the car, spoke before he could. "It's okay, Tommy. She's the robbery victim's daughter."

Helma Zukas did not ride elevators unless there was absolutely no alternative. In the lobby of the Silver Gables, she passed the elevator and turned the corner to push open the heavy steel fire door. She took the stairs two at a time.

"I'm going to join a gym, I swear I am," Ruth gasped behind her, her labored breathing echoing in the stairwell.

"Daily walking on varied terrain provides all the stamina necessary," Helma distractedly informed Ruth as she pulled open the door to the fourth floor. Both her breath and her heart pulsed as steadily as if she had simply climbed the outside stairs of the Bayside Arms to her third-floor apartment.

Policemen were gathered in the fourth-floor hallway, serious-faced, speaking quietly. Farther down the hall, she could see her mother and Aunt Em's door standing open. Other apartment doors gaped ajar, too, and residents watched from doorways or chatted together at a cautious distance.

"Mrs. Caldecott." Helma acknowledged the woman standing outside the apartment next to her mother's, tight black jeans encasing her plump body, pink plastic curlers in her hair, and a barbecue apron tied around her waist that read, *Too Hot for You.*

"Did you see the body?" Mrs. Caldecott asked, reaching out to touch Helma's arm. Her eyes shone behind her glasses, and her voice sounded *excited*. Her eyebrows rose and lowered as if it were a trick question.

Helma stopped midstride and Ruth nearly ran into her. "No."

"Come in here, then," Mrs. Caldecott beckoned. "You can look out my window." She glanced toward Helma's mother's apartment and held her hand to the side of her mouth, whispering. "I have a better view, and they moved the TV off him so now you can really see what's what."

When an unexpected opportunity presented itself, Helma believed it was prudent to consider it seriously, especially when it might prove to be the only opportunity.

"Thank you, Mrs. Caldecott. May I?"

The older woman's smile widened. "This way. It's not often you get to see a crime right in front of your eyes. You think when you get old and live in a place like this, that you're only going to see old people die. But no," She paused. That *was* excitement in her voice. "Violence follows you everywhere."

"Mary had a little lamb," Ruth recited, apropos of nothing.

"You're so right," Mrs. Caldecott agreed.

Mrs. Caldecott's apartment was jam-packed with furniture and knickknacks that appeared to be souvenirs from around the world. Her walls were covered with framed photographs, each one sporting a white stick-on label.

"Over here," Mrs. Caldecott said, waving her arm toward the single window in her living room.

Helma peered down through the window, Ruth gazing over her shoulder. And there it was. Four stories below, policemen milled around a body lying in the Silver Gables parking lot. Her mother's television set lay beside the body, shards of glass glistening in the sun.

"Told ya," Ruth murmured.

"Carrie was lucky she'd already left for her hair appointment. That's her space," Mrs. Caldecott said from behind Helma. "And look how close he came to Mr. Paine's car. He loves that old Cadillac. Washes and waxes it every Saturday. He took me to the grocery store in it once."

The body belonged to a man in his late twenties or early thirties, with short brown hair, wearing jeans and a black jacket with the sleeves pushed up. He lay on his stomach, his face to the side, one hand outstretched toward the television. He may have had a tattoo; Helma couldn't make out whether that was a design on his lower arm or a smear of dirt.

"Would you happen to have a pair of binoculars I might borrow?" Helma asked Mrs. Caldecott.

"Right beside you, dear," she said, pointing to the windowsill.

Next to a framed photo of a man holding a large pinkish fish that Helma noted was a sockeye salmon past its prime, and labeled only "Him," sat a pair of black binoculars. Helma peered through them, adjusting the sights and aiming toward the parking lot beneath her. She gasped at the magnified scene, jerking her view away from the blood pooled near the dead man's head. Yes, late twenties. She'd seen bodies before and while she wasn't shocked, she felt the wash of sadness at life ended too soon.

"Hardly worth a TV," Ruth commented.

The tattoo was partially obscured by the angle of his arm to the window, but Helma glimpsed the red and blue hues common to tattoo artists.

"Do you know who he is?" she asked Mrs. Caldecott.

Mrs. Caldecott ducked beneath Ruth's arm and pressed her forehead to the glass, gazing down at the scene. "Never seen him before. They're saying Em pushed him out the window." She shook her head. "It's hard to believe, a young healthy man like that. Just look at the size of those thighs – and her such a little thing."

"Adrenalin is a wondrous hormone," Ruth told her.

Mrs. Caldecott nodded sagely and patted one of her pink plastic curlers. "Oh, yes. Don't I know that."

Helma had seen all she could of the body and turned the binoculars on the gathering policemen. Solemn faces, jotting in notebooks, one policeman speaking into a cellphone. The chief of police wasn't among them. No doubt he soon would be.

She removed a clean tissue from her left pocket and wiped the eyepieces of the binoculars and returned them to the windowsill. "Thank you, Mrs. Caldecott. We'll join my mother and aunt in their apartment now."

"They'll have quite the story," Mrs. Caldecott said as she escorted them to the door. "I can't wait to hear the details at Gin and Rummy Club tonight."

"Hi, Sid," Ruth said to the blond policeman standing in Lillian and Aunt Em's doorway. "Got it figured out?"

"Ruth, Miss Zukas," he acknowledged, disregarding Ruth's question. "Your mother's been asking if you'd arrived yet."

Helma had known Sidney Lehman since he first joined the Bellehaven Police Department, and although their paths had crossed in strictly police matters, Ruth and Sidney's paths had intersected in matters Helma felt it was wiser not to explore.

Behind Sidney, in the apartment's living room, Aunt Em and Lillian sat side by side on the sofa, Helma's mother holding Aunt Em's hands in both her own. It was a rare display of affection between the oft-bickering sisters-in-law, and Helma savored the sight for a moment before entering the room.

Aunt Em was Helma's father's oldest sister, the last one alive of that big—both in size and numbers - raucous Lithuanian family. Lillian had moved to Bellehaven after Helma's father's death, Aunt Em a few years later. And while she and Lillian had finally resolved years of animosity and forged a mainly amicable existence, Helma would never dare tell the two women that despite their age difference, they were beginning to resemble one another.

Lillian raised her head and spotted Helma. "Oh. You're here at last." She glanced behind Helma and added, "Oh. Hello, Ruth."

"Wilhelmina, Ruthie," Aunt Em said in her Lithuanian accent, which grew thicker as she grew older, as if English were becoming the foreign language and she was reverting to her native tongue. Her thin hair was mussed, circles of pink high-lighted her cheeks. "I murdered a robber."

Lillian patted and rubbed Aunt Em's hand. "No no, Em. You did not kill him. He jumped." She glared at Helma and Ruth and the police, daring anyone to disagree with her.

Aunt Em pulled back and squinted into Helma's mother's face. "He was doing a…killing himself? He was afraid of me and jumped out the window?"

"Of course not." Lillian laughed a single laugh. "The sight of you surprised him so much he tried to escape. He was caught and he knew the only future left for him was jail. He went a lit-tle crazy and forgot where he was and thought the window was a door, that's all."

Aunt Em frowned doubtfully. A policewoman handed her a glass of water and murmured a few words in a soothing tone. Voices came from the rear of the apartment: men's voices. More policemen.

"Did he hurt you, Aunt Em?" Helma asked, bending to kiss Aunt Em's cheek.

"He did not touch me. I was napping and I hear a noise, so out I come to look. And here he is"—she pointed to the space in front of the sofa – "holding our TV. He cursed when he saw me." She shook her head sadly, moving her lips as if mouthing his words.

"Tut, tut," Lillian soothed. "At least he didn't injure you. If only I hadn't run down to watch the ping-pong finals, I would have been here to stop him from coming in."

"You think he would have been too afraid of *you* to come inside?" Aunt Em asked.

Helma heard the inflection of challenge in her voice. "If he'd known you were here, Aunt Em," she said, "I'm sure he wouldn't have entered your apartment at all."

"Weird for a robber to choose this place," Ruth said, gazing around the apartment.

Exactly what Helma was thinking. A thief choosing to rob a retirement home on a Sunday afternoon? Two policemen stood in the dining area in front of the broken window that overlooked the parking lot. Glass clung in jagged shards to the frame. One of the officers was speaking into a small recorder, and both gazed down at the floor.

Their legs blocked Helma's view of whatever they were studying, so she stepped closer to them. "Excuse me, please," she said. Neither moved, but one shifted far enough to expose a carving knife lying on the carpet.

It was a knife that normally protruded handle-end out from the oak holder on the counter. The knife holder had been a present from Helma after she noticed her mother dropping knives willy-nilly into a cabinet drawer.

The blade appeared clean, unstained by blood. Whatever had happened, at least no one had actually *used* the knife.

"Now there's an interesting piece of evidence," Ruth said quietly, nodding toward the knife on the floor. "Your aunt's luckier than we realized."

Helma agreed, wondering if the robber had threatened Aunt Em. Or had Aunt Em threatened the robber?

"I'm Camella Gardener," the policewoman who'd given Aunt Em the glass of water, said to Helma. "I'd like to ask your aunt a few questions." Officer Gardener was a buxom woman, with thick dark hair and a round, cozy face. When she spoke, her melodious voice exuded a soothing everything's-going-to-be-just-fine aura.

"I'd prefer to be present during any questioning," Helma told her.

"Definitely." Camella sat down in the chair opposite Aunt Em, holding a pen and spiral notebook. She smiled "Can you describe the robber for me?"

"Just look out the window," Aunt Em told her. "That's him. He has a tattoo." She touched her arm in the same area where Helma had seen a portion of the man's tattoo. "He was a thug."

"Do you have to grill her now?" Lillian asked, her voice rising a notch. "She's had a shock and she's ol...fragile."

"Hmmph." Aunt Em stiffened and tugged her hand from Lillian's.

"I know," the policewoman told Lillian in her soothing voice. "And I'm sorry. It's always best to ask these hard questions when the event's fresh. Sometimes, later..."

Aunt Em nodded and said cheerfully, "My memory's not so good as a year ago." And now Lillian "Hmmph"ed.

"I'll be as quick as I can," Camella said. She included both women in her glance, sounding apologetic, as if they held all the power, not her.

"Knock, knock," a man's voice interrupted from the door.

Kenneth Vine, the manager of the Silver Gables, stood in the open doorway. Behind him, two white-haired women peered into the apartment. He was a red-faced, hearty man whom Helma had often seen joking with the female residents. Beside Helma, Ruth muttered, "Uh oh, a comb-over."

"I'm totally shocked this crime was perpetrated here," he boomed, rubbing his hands together, glancing around to include everyone in the room. "We've never had a robbery in our complex.

Never once." He spotted Helma and his eyebrows rose, not exactly in friendly acknowledgement. More often than she'd anticipated since Lillian and Aunt Em had moved into the Silver Gables, Helma had taken a moment during her visits to remind him of a manager's responsibilities to his tenants.

Chief of Police Wayne Gallant emerged from the rear of the apartment. The sudden awareness that he'd been inside the apartment the entire time she'd been present was disconcerting, as if she should have somehow been conscious of his presence, that she should have *known*.

He nodded to Helma, smiling, and she felt the corners of her mouth helplessly rise. Ruth elbowed her and Helma moved a discreet step away. The chief appeared rested, relaxed. He was a tall man whose graying hair formed a widow's peak he often allowed his hair to fall forward and cover. It was definitely not the same as a comb-over.

"Ken," the chief acknowledged the manager. "You have surveillance cameras, right?"

Kenneth Vine's head bobbed. "Sure, chief. In the elevators and the lobby."

"Not the hallways?"

The manager's face flushed redder. His eyes darted between the policemen. "Usually. Four and three have been out a couple of weeks. Some of our residents call them 'Big Brother' and snip the wires. I meant to have them fixed, but they just cut the wires again. Think they're being spied on."

It was no secret that the Silver Gables had a reputation for being the preferred complex for more "active" seniors.

Wayne didn't comment. "Somebody must have seen this guy." He nodded toward the window. "He would have looked out-of-place sneaking around the complex."

The manager had at first responded nervously, but now his voice sharpened in defensiveness. "I don't know. The Silver

Gables isn't an institution. People come and go. We don't monitor arrivals and departures."

"Which is exactly why," Ruth said in a low voice, "this place has the reputation it has."

"Do you know who he is?" Lillian asked the chief. "Em said she didn't recognize him."

"We don't have an identification yet," Wayne told her.

"Why did he want to rob us?" she continued. "We're not rich."

"And now he's a dead duck," Aunt Em added.

Wayne turned to Aunt Em, "I know this is upsetting, ma'am, but his fall wasn't your fault."

"It was, too," Aunt Em raised her head and met the chief's eyes. "I did it."

"Now, Em," Lillian soothed. "You did not."

Wayne gestured to Sidney Lehman. "Question every resident about strangers in the building today. And Ken, we'll look at the surveillance tapes you do have. I'd suggest you get the cameras fixed."

"I will. No problem. I'll call Landy's Security right now."

Wayne turned his attention back to Lillian and Em, hunkering in front of them and resting his elbows on his knees. "Whatever your burglar managed to pocket before you surprised him, we should find on his body, but can you look through the apartment with Officer Gardner here," he nodded to the policewoman named Camella, who smiled up at him, "and tell her what's missing."

"Let's start in your bedrooms," Camella suggested as she helped Aunt Em rise from the sofa. Helma's mother rose, too, and waved her hand toward the dining table. "At least he didn't steal my computer. I'd be lost without it." On the table where Helma usually sat when she dined with Lillian and Aunt Em, a stack of computer manuals sat beside a white laptop. "Just lost," she continued, shaking her head. "I'm surprised he didn't grab it before that TV set. I don't know what I would have done. My files are irreplaceable."

Helma's mother had purchased the computer a month earlier and had embraced the technology, signing up for ever more classes, buying special computer eyeglasses, and now plotting to hold her own classes to instruct any "backward" residents of the Silver Gables. "Don't Let Your Grandkids Leave You in the Dust!" read one of her sign-up sheets pinned to the lobby bulletin board. "Let me know if I can help you with library questions," she'd told Helma, and avidly scouted out conversational lapses to chronicle tales of her internet prowess.

While Ruth zeroed in on Sidney, asking him, "You ever find that shirt?" Helma followed after her mother and Aunt Em, who leaned heavily on Camella's arm.

Aunt Em's room, since she'd emerged from it to surprise the burglar mid-robbery, hadn't been touched. In Lillian's room, a mound of tangled jewelry sparkled in the middle of her bed and her wooden jewelry box lay tipped on its side on the floor, open.

"The snake," Aunt Em said, her favorite epithet, only surprisingly in English instead of Lithuanian.

"Oh my." Lillian sat on the bed by the jewelry, already sorting. "My good earrings are gone," Her voice faltered as she rummaged through the puddle of earrings, necklaces and pins, her hands shaking. "They were real pearls. My opal ring's gone. It's genuine, too. You know, opals are bad luck if they're not your birthstone, unless somebody gives them to you, that is." She chattered at high speed. "You can't buy opals for yourself— that'll bring the worst luck. The ring was a gift but now it's been taken so maybe it wasn't too good of luck, anyway, was it?"

"Not for the opal," Aunt Em said.

"Oh," Lillian moaned and slumped over the tangle. "My ring." She fingered frantically through the silver pins and gold chains and mostly costume jewelry, picking up pieces and dropping them, squinting at each bit of shine. "My wedding ring. I mean, it wasn't very valuable. In fact, it was the cheapest ring we could find. We didn't have any money for anything nicer." Still pawing, in more agitation, her voice rising. "I can't wear it anymore because of the arthritis. It wasn't worth much, really. Your father said he'd buy me another one, but..."

And she raised her hands to her cheeks and burst into tears.

"Oh, Lil," Aunt Em soothed and put her arms around the younger woman, pulling her head closer as if she were a child. Lillian sobbed on Aunt Em's shoulder. Helma patted her mother's arm.

"I'm sorry, Mother, but the police will recover it. I'm sure your ring is on the bod... scene. It was probably in his pocket."

Camella raised her head from her notebook. "If you give me a detailed description, I'll personally look for it," she told Lillian, even smiling.

Besides Helma's mother's jewelry, a gold-rimmed porcelain angel was missing, a set of four silver iced-tea spoons—"I thought people only stole silverware in old mysteries," Ruth commented—and a small bronze plaque naming Lillian "Member of the Year" from her VFW Auxiliary days in Michigan.

"Very few items were taken, actually," Camella said as she held Aunt Em's elbow and ushered her back to the sofa.

"Because I interrupted him and killed him," Aunt Em reminded Camella.

"Yes, but he *touched* our things, Em" Lillian said. "He invaded our privacy. It was an assault."

Wayne stood near the window, and added as if he'd been pondering their conversation, "Every item was small except for the television. Do you have insurance?" he asked Lillian.

"Of course, Lillian replied. "*I'm* careful about insurance," and Helma knew what was coming next: the story of her father and his mythical life insurance policy.

"Take one last look around out here in the living room," Helma hurriedly suggested, hoping to forestall reawakening a grudge against the dead, "before the police leave."

Aunt Em and Lillian slowly circled the small apartment, heads turning, examining high and low. At the imitation fire-place—not even gas but only the rippling electrical illusion of flame—Aunt Em suddenly raised her hand and tapped an empty spot on the mantel. "My *Stelmužė* box," she cried out in a cracked voice. "My *Stelmužė* box."

"What's that?" Wayne asked, turning at the timbre of Aunt Em's cry. He left the window where he'd been viewing the scene in the parking lot below and joined Aunt Em.

"My *Stelmužė* box," Aunt Em repeated. "It's gone."

He turned to Helma for clarification but she couldn't recall what had been sitting on the mantel, and she was unfamiliar with the Lithuanian word, *Stelmužė*. They both turned to Helma's mother for translation.

Lillian made a shape in the air with her hands, a rectangle slightly larger than a deck of cards. "It was a carved box. Wood, with designs cut into it."

"My *papa*," Aunt Em whispered, still gazing at the empty spot on the mantel, her face stricken.

Helma remembered the little box, intricately carved with geometric designs in the Lithuanian tradition, so dense that from a distance it resembled a weaving.

"What was inside it, Aunt Em?" Helma asked. "Jewelry?"

Aunt Em shook her head. "No, no. It was from Papa. He made it for me," Her voice caught. "With his knife."

"He carved it?"

"Oh, Em," Lillian said. "It's from your past. And he stole from my past, too. The robber burgled our past."

Camella's hand rested on Aunt Em's back. And now she raised her other hand to touch Lillian's shoulder.

"Wait a second," Ruth broke in. "None of it's really *gone*. Like Helma said, your jewelry and the box are on the dead guy's body." She shrugged. "Well, unless they got smashed in the fall, anyway."

She'd only made it worse. Aunt Em and Lillian peered at each other, teary-eyed and lost. Lillian dabbed at her eyes and Aunt Em's chin trembled. The apartment was filled with sorrow so palpable that everyone, including the police and Helma, stood paralyzed by the intensity of it, all eyes on the two weeping women.

"Do something," Ruth hissed at her, "before this devolves into one big crying jag."

Helma noted the shiny eyes of Camella, felt the scratch at the back of her own throat. The chief tipped his head and gazed at Aunt Em and Lillian as if he were a small boy puzzled by how to fix a grown-up problem.

Ruth rolled her eyes and brought her hands together in a startlingly loud clap. "Guess what, everybody," she said, her big voice shattering the silence. "You will not guess, never ever, not in a million years."

Like a ringmaster, she bowed and held out one long arm toward Wayne. "Our very own chief of police here, the gallant Wayne Gallant, and..." Now she turned and bowed, waving her other arm just as ceremoniously toward Helma, "public librarian beloved by throngs of Bellehavenites, Miss Helma Zukas..." She inhaled a deep breath and announced in the same tones appropriate in presenting a death-defying high-wire act.

"...Are getting married."

CHAPTER 3

Great Expectations

It was as if a cosmic toggle had been thrown, Helma thought later.

Grief and loss flew out the window, replaced by a chorus of gasps, and shrieks of joy from Helma's mother. Aunt Em's trembling lips stilled and a smile widened her face as she pressed her hands to her heart. Even the other police officers stared first at the chief, then at Helma.

The robbery, the missing items, the carving knife on the floor, not to mention the dead man on the parking lot pavement four floors below, had all been relegated to Old News.

Ruth benignly observed the excitement, her face smug at the diversion she'd created. She gracefully pirouetted on her three-inch heels to capture the full effect on the faces of everyone in the room, looking as if she were prepared to curtsy to applause. Helma caught Wayne's eye and held his gaze, the two of them occupying a mental island of calm.

"Oh, Billie," her mother breathed, slipping back into the childish nickname Helma hadn't heard since she'd forbidden its use when she was nine. "Oh, oh. At last." She dabbed at her eyes. "A wedding."

"Love," Aunt Em whispered, and sighed, hands still clasped to her heart.

"Congratulations," the policewoman said, not looking at Helma or Wayne, her voice distinctly lacking in enthusiasm.

"Cool," added a young policeman's bored voice.

"I need my computer," Lillian said, turning toward the dining room table. "We have to make lists. There's so much to do before... before when, Helma? When's the date?"

"I..." Helma began

"And a dress. Oh, I wish I hadn't loaned mine to that Spenser girl who married your cousin Ricky. I clearly told her it was only a loan, not that that made any difference. And now they're divorced and who knows where my dress is, let alone her—not me, that's for sure. Not even Ricky." She shook her head. "Well, that can't be helped now, can it? Rose on the fifth floor used to have a bridal shop. She can recommend a boutique in Bellehaven. Well, we may have to go to Seattle. Or Vancouver. I have all of last year's *Bride* magazines under my bed. We can look through those for ideas."

"*Bride* magazine?" Helma asked. "You have copies of *Bride* magazine?"

"And who will be your maid of honor?" Lillian hastily asked. She glanced at Ruth and instantly away, saying, "Flowers. Orchids are nice. I always wanted orchids."

Helma's eyelids lowered as if weights were attached to her lashes. She held up her hand. "We'll talk later, Mother. I'll come back after the police are finished."

"But—"

"Right," Ruth interjected, her smile still too self-satisfied. "We'll run down, take a little peek at the crime scene and be back in a sec." And when the chief took a step toward them, his mouth working soundlessly, Ruth gave him a brilliant smile and said to Lillian in a honeyed voice, "You can discuss the details with the chie...your soon-to-be son-in-law, here."

Wayne's mouth opened, then closed as Helma's mother giggled in delight and gazed wide-eyed up at Wayne. "Wayne," she breathed. "We do have a lot to discuss, don't we? I have some old pictures of Helma. She was the cutest thing. Who would have thought…"

"Come on," Ruth muttered, nudging Helma. "Dead bodies are preferable to this."

They slipped out the apartment door and Helma glanced back, a pang of sympathy for Wayne as he gamely but uncertainly leaned toward her mother.

"Thank you, I think," she told Ruth, Wayne Gallant's face as he fell victim to her mother's enthusiasm fresh in her mind. She certainly wasn't abandoning him, not at all. He was investigating a crime on the premises; it was where he needed to be.

"You *should* thank me," Ruth said over her shoulder. "I lifted everybody's spirits, didn't I?"

"You complicated the situation," Helma told her bluntly. "The robbery is enough to—"

"Nah, I transformed a miserable situation into a happy one. Ponder for a moment how my little announcement shifted thoughts of gloom into…" Ruth spread her arms, "visions of marital bliss."

Helma recalled her mother's eager, glowing face—and felt her own heart sinking.

Ruth clattered down the four flights of stairs ahead of Helma, flashing a smile at a blond maintenance man carrying a bucket and mop. "Oughta take the elevator," she told him.

"Too many people going up and down in all the excitement," he said, wheezing.

"Almost there," she told him cheerily.

At the lobby level, Ruth pushed open the fire door and they faced the knots of mostly white-haired people in the lounge who'd turned at the sound of the opening door. "What'll we do now?" she asked Helma.

"I'd like to view the body."

"Why?" Ruth stopped. "I only said we'd take a look for effect. Let's go to the Web Locker across the street until the police leave. We'll sit by the window so we can watch."

"I prefer to do this," Helma told her. She led the way through the lobby toward the front doors, stopping once to assure a bald man in a wheelchair that no, the ambulance wasn't there to pick him up.

"Sunday afternoon is an unusual time to commit a robbery of two elderly women in a retirement center," she told Ruth.

"So? Leave this one to our city's finest, Helm."

"*Helma*," she corrected absently. "I'm merely curious, that's all. I don't intend to interfere with police business."

"Right." Ruth guffawed unnecessarily. "But it *is* weird. Fourth floor and all that. Not exactly like he could lug a load of loot out their door and down four floors, stuff it in his trunk and hit the freeway without anybody noticing."

"Exactly. And why Aunt Em and my mother? Whatever they own has more sentimental than monetary value." Helma halted at the ribbon of yellow police tape, which surely kept the public farther from the scene than was necessary.

"Maybe their apartment was the first one the guy could duck into without being seen." Ruth shrugged. "You don't really believe your Aunt Em scared him out the window?"

"There was a knife on the floor." Aunt Em had once stabbed a potential purse snatcher with a hat pin. "She's had her fierce moments."

"That old adrenalin thing again."

Helma peered around a tall, beige-jacketed couple, angling for a better view of the body, which had yet to be removed, or even covered. The victim's face was turned away and the broken television blocked her sight of the tattoo.

A slight breeze had risen, sending a candy wrapper skittering past the robber's feet. He wore black high-top canvas shoes.

"Excuse me," Helma told the couple, and ducked beneath the yellow do-not-cross tape.

"I hate it when you do this," Ruth said, remaining behind the line.

"Ma'am," a dark-haired policeman warned, stepping in front of Helma and positioning his arms out from his sides to block her route.

"I'm sorry," Helma said, using the silver-dime-in-ice-water voice she'd developed to settle unruly library patrons and unfettered children, "but it was my mother's apartment the victim fell from, and I may be able to identify him."

He didn't move, although a muscle clearly jumped in his jaw.

"Unless you already have identified the body," she said casually. "In that case, I'll tell Chief Gallant he has no need for my assistance."

His eyes shifted just perceptibly. Anyone less observant than Helma Zukas wouldn't have noticed. She stepped neatly beyond the reach of his outstretched arms and around him. "Thank you for your cooperation," she told him, smiling.

From the police line she heard Ruth telling the beige couple, "That's right, and she'll soon be Mrs. Police Chief Gallant."

As she'd surmised by her examination through Mrs. Caldecott's binoculars, the man was in his late twenties. Closer, he appeared young, childish almost, with a turned-up nose and freshly-shaven face. His eyes were half-closed and his lips parted, exposing the edge of a chipped front tooth. Blood pooled in a dark arc beneath his cheek.

Helma glanced away from his face. There was nothing familiar about him. He didn't appear to be a library regular, and lacked the features she associated with avid readers. She noted his worn sneakers and faded jeans, the shiny black jacket

Another step closer and she had a clear view of the tattoo above his wrist: a crude red heart, the center smudged where there'd once been a name or initials.

"He may be a former prisoner," Helma said to the young policeman who hovered at her elbow, poised to tug her away from the body the instant she misbehaved.

"Then you recognize him?" he asked, a touch of surprise inflecting his question.

"I'm not sure yet," she said, wishing to spend a few more minutes examining the man, "I've read that many tattoo artists learn their craft while residing in our judicial system. His tattoo has an amateurish cast, doesn't it?"

He tipped his head and bent to view the tattoo more closely, but didn't comment.

"Have the stolen items been recovered yet? Jewelry and a small carved box? Also a small figurine and silver teaspoons?"

"You'll have to ask somebody else, ma'am." He nodded toward the dead man. "*Do* you recognize him?" he asked again.

Helma had seen all she could without moving the body, and she doubted the young policeman would stand by while she did *that*. "No, I'm sorry, I don't," and then added, "But I appreciate your cooperation," and made her way back to the police line where Ruth waited. As she ducked beneath the yellow tape, two men in light blue wheeled a gurney toward the body. Neatly folded on the gurney lay a black plastic bag.

Wayne stepped from the side door of the Silver Gables, frowning at the sight of Helma exiting the cordoned area.

"I was unable to identify him," Helma told him. "He's not a library user."

He grinned at her. "You could tell that?"

"Not a Bellehaven Public Library user," she clarified, wondering why he *still* grinned at her. "About the items stolen from my mother and Aunt Em..."

"Bring the two of them to the station tomorrow morning so they can identify what we recover."

"Were other apartments robbed, too?" He stood three feet from Helma, totally professional, but she caught a whiff of the same cologne he'd been wearing the evening before. She cleared her throat. "Were there more objects on his body than Mother and Aunt Em reported stolen?"

"Possibly. Although he doesn't look overladen with stolen goods, does he?"

"Unless he cached the articles somewhere in the building."

He nodded, considering her. "We're searching the building now. He didn't have time to hide anything from your mother's apartment." He touched Helma's shoulder, lightly, hardly noticeable if she hadn't been looking right at him, but unaccountably, Helma felt a curious… buzz course through her body. It wasn't unpleasant.

"Aunt Em won't be entangled in this, will she? Despite what she believes, there's absolutely no way she could have pushed a man his size out the window. She doesn't have the strength."

Ruth cleared her throat and Helma added, "Even accounting for adrenalin."

"It's unlikely," Wayne agreed. He frowned at the men handling the gurney, who appeared to be holding a sociable conversation. One of the men laughed and Wayne's eyes narrowed.

"We'll talk to her again." He turned his Baltic blue eyes on Helma, "but I'm guessing the thief thought he was alone. The sight of her probably startled him and he backed away from her."

"Holding the television skewed his balance?" Helma suggested.

He nodded. "That's my opinion." He touched his forehead to her and slipped beneath the tape.

"There's something funny here," Ruth said. She watched Wayne stalking toward the two EMTs, the tip of her pinky fingernail between her teeth.

"You don't mean humorous, do you?" There was no accounting for what Ruth might find funny. The EMT who'd been laughing stood at attention as Wayne spoke to him, standing uncomfortably close.

"Of course not. At least not yet, anyway. Odd."

"Crimes are usually unfathomable to the average citizen."

Ruth shrugged. "I just don't buy it, that a criminal was so traumatized by the sight of a nearly ninety-year-old woman still groggy from sleep, that he crashed through a closed fourth floor window and fell to his death."

"And your theory is?" Helma asked.

"Don't know, but it's something else."

CHAPTER 4

The Distant Landscape

Aunt Em and Lillian sat at their dining room table, Aunt Em holding a cup of tea and Lillian tapping furiously on her computer keyboard.

"Do you have our things?" Helma's mother demanded the instant Helma and Ruth entered, peering over the rims of her computer glasses at them.

"Tomorrow morning we'll go to the police station so you can identify the items they recovered," Helma told her.

"I can identify them right now," Lillian said indignantly.

"I know, but the police need to record them for the case."

"Hmmph. It's not like they're going to charge him," and she went back to her computer, fingers flying, eyes intense.

"What are you writing, Mother?" Helma asked.

"An account of the incident. For the Gin and Rummy Club newsletter. And for all my friends, too."

"Not her real friends," Aunt Em said. "Not the ones who live and breathe in front of you. For her friends on ..." She waved a hand to the computer.

Helma knew her mother had joined Facebook and every online social group she felt pertained to her interests, including boxing, model railroading, miniature-rose growing, romance readers, makeup lovers, and something called "Widows Speak Up."

Aunt Em made pushing motions with her hands. 'I hope he didn't break anything."

"Your little gold angel will definitely be shattered," Lillian told her, lifting her hands from her keyboard with a flourish.

"But not my *Stelmužė* box. Papa made it good and strong."

Lillian nodded absently and settled back in her chair, one hand still hovering protectively over her computer keyboard. "Now Helma, we *must* talk about your wedding. Have you considered the guest list? Wouldn't it be fun to combine it with a family reunion, so everyone could see...I mean, meet, your new husband, our chief of police? If only your father could give you away."

"My Juozas can do it," Aunt Em said, then at the look on their faces, shook her head. "He's gone, isn't he?"

Lillian and Helma exchanged startled glances, Aunt Em's husband, Juozas, had been dead thirty years, but Ruth suddenly leaned down and smacked a loud kiss on top of Aunt Em's head. "Dead as a doornail," she said cheerfully. "Years ago."

Lillian frowned and bit her lip, and Helma braced herself for Aunt Em to burst into tears, but her aunt chuckled and patted Ruth's hand. "Thank you, Ruthie."

"Wayne and I haven't begun making wedding plans yet, Mother," Helma warned her mother. "But we'll want a small..."

"At your age, dear, not that I'm criticizing, but anything small would be a waste."

Then, uncharacteristically, her mother suddenly tipped her head as if glimpsing a landscape that hadn't quite come into sight around an upcoming corner, gave Helma a distant smile and abruptly abandoned the topic of weddings. She waved her hand toward the broken window and said in a calm—too calm – voice. "Now isn't the time to talk weddings, I suppose, not with crime and death walking in the door."

"And right out the window," Ruth added.

"Because of me," Aunt Em said softly.

"Aunt Em, do you remember the carving knife?" Helma asked.

"You can borrow it."

"No, thank you, but the police found it on the floor after the robbery. Do you remember that?"

"Helma," her mother admonished. "Not now."

Aunt Em frowned. Behind her glasses her eyes sagged in fatigue. "The carving knife? I don't remember that."

The manager, Kenneth Vine, returned with two men in gray coveralls. *Jenter's Glass* was stitched on their pockets. Neither man acknowledged the women, concentrating on maneuvering a pane of glass in a wooden frame through the door.

"We'll get you girls fixed right up," the manager told Lillian and Aunt Em. "You'll never even know there was an...accident, here."

"Girls?" Ruth asked, her eyes flashing, but Lillian giggled and said, "Oh, we don't mind."

Ruth rolled her eyes.

"Did you discover the robber's image on your security cameras?" Helma asked.

The manager shifted his eyes from Helma to the pane of glass. "The police have everything that was available," he said vaguely. "Now about this window. Would you *ladies*," he emphasized the word and paused to look at Ruth, who shook her head at him, "like to go out for lunch while we fix this? On the house, naturally."

"Yes," Lillian said. "We'd love to."

"I'm going to watch," Aunt Em told him, "to be sure it's a good job."

"That's not necessary, Em," Lillian argued. She smiled at the manager. "They're *professionals*."

"I'm staying," Aunt Em asserted.

Lillian heaved a sigh and surrendered. "I suppose I'll have to stay here with her, then."

The men jockeyed the glass around the table toward the broken window and leaned it against the wall.

"Just a sec," Ruth told them and stepped to the window to gaze down at the parking lot. "All cleaned up," she announced, "just like it was all a cheap magic trick." She touched a finger to a shard of glass stuck in the window frame and turned away.

Suddenly Aunt Em gasped and held up the big-dialed wristwatch Helma had given her for Christmas. "The funeral. I forgot. Am I too late to go to the funeral?"

"Whose funeral?" Helma asked.

"Rimas Klimas," Aunt Em told her. "He died three days ago."

Ruth tipped her head and whispered "Rimas Klimas" twice, as if it were a child's nursery rhyme.

"Who is he?" Helma asked

"Wait," Lillian said, holding up her left hand while she clicked keys with her right. "He's a member of Em's Lithuanian club." She worked her mouse and squinted close to the monitor. "Mm-hmm," she murmured. "Almost there. Here we go. Got it." Then she read from the screen: "Klimas, Rimas Antanas. 415 15th Street...Immigrated to the United States in 1949." She counted off on her fingers. "He died at the age 87."

She looked up, her smile wide. "Isn't that wonderful. Just that quick," and she snapped her fingers.

"I could have said the words faster," Aunt Em told her. "I knew that."

"You've listed the members of Aunt Em's Lithuanian club on your computer?" Helma asked.

"In their own file," Lillian proudly tapped the edge of her computer. "I have a file for everyone in the building. And all your librarians, too. Just ask me." She poised her hands over the keyboard, waiting, expectantly looking at Helma.

"No thank you," Helma told her. "Is it too late for Aunt Em to attend the funeral? I can take her. But are you sure the funeral's not tomorrow, or Tuesday? Today's Sunday. Usually..."

"It was so his family could be here," Aunt Em said. "They come from far away."

Lillian glanced at the wall clock. "It started twenty minutes ago."

"I'm sorry, Aunt Em. Was he a friend of yours?"

Aunt Em shrugged. "He was a DP," she said, "but he was my fellow countryman. I only knew him a little while. Is okay."

A DP was a Displaced Person who came to the United States after World War II. A subtle—and sometimes not-so-subtle - bias existed between the earlier and later immigrants.

Aunt Em's Lithuanian club was a year old, part of a move to reclaim roots, or as Ruth said, "throw some lumps into the melting pot."

The club's mostly elderly members met once a month where they ate Lithuanian food and sang Lithuanian songs. Aunt Em worked for days before a meeting baking *kugelis* and bacon buns and Little Ear pastries. Each time Aunt Em returned from a meeting, Lillian confided in Helma, "She's broody. Too much looking backward. It's not healthy for old people."

"Are you meeting your fiancé now?" Lillian asked, pausing lovingly over the word fiancé. "You two have so much to discuss."

"He's very busy at the moment, Mother. If you're all right, I'll go home, and tomorrow I'll phone you when the police are ready with your stolen goods."

"The loot," Aunt Em said.

"All you'll have to do is identify the items and you can bring them home."

Aunt Em struggled up from her chair, using both hands. She tried to pull her shoulders straight and failed, her tiny figure slumping, then, after successfully maneuvering herself out of the chair, followed Ruth and Helma to the apartment door. "When will be this wedding?" she asked Helma, glancing back at Lillian whose gaze was riveted on her computer screen. Helma had witnessed that unblinking, dazed expression on the faces of hundreds of library patrons. Her mother was oblivious.

"We haven't decided, Aunt Em. Maybe next summer."

"That far away?"

"We have a lot to plan," Helma told her.

"Will you be happy?"

"I believe so."

"That is good. But a year is a long time. Can love wait so long?"

A chill passed through Helma and she took Aunt Em's hand. Her skin was soft, like fingering the silkiest and sheerest of fabrics. "You have to help me plan, Aunt Em. I'll need your advice."

"Ah, I don't know weddings." She sighed, pressing against Helma. "But I do know love."

"Dead people upset *me*," Ruth said as they drove toward the Slope, where Ruth lived in a converted carriage house. She waved her arm out the window to a man on a bicycle who veered into the car lane in his effort to adequately return her wave, causing a screech of brakes and angry honks. "But that dead guy barely made a ripple in your mother and aunt's life. They were more interested in your upcoming nuptials."

"Wasn't that your intent when you told them, to take their minds off the dead robber?"

"Don't go all reasonable on me." Ruth rubbed her nose. "Maybe that's just what happens when you get old: death becomes one of life's mundanities, like arthritis and false teeth."

"Aunt Em said once that death begins to look more like a friend when you're older." Again Helma experienced the chill she'd felt in her mother's apartment.

"Mm," Ruth said, and then, "Have you thought of lime green?"

"For Aunt Em?"

Ruth rolled her eyes. "You definitely *are* going to need help."

CHAPTER 5

Looking for an Opening

After Helma parked her car and double checked to be sure her doors were locked, she looked up to see TNT leaning on the railing of the third floor landing of the Bayside Arms, between his apartment, 3E, and Helma's, 3F.

Each of the three floors of the Bayside Arms had outside landings across the front, like a 1980s motel. Separate balconies jutted from every apartment on the water side of the building, giving residents "killer views" of Washington Bay and the San Juan Islands.

TNT waved, straightened, and, dressed in his usual sweats, bounded down to meet her on the first landing, a white towel around his neck.

"I heard about it," the retired boxer said. He ran a hand through his wiry gray hair and down his craggy jaw, which was in need of shaving. "Is she all right?"

Helma knew by "she" he meant her mother. TNT and Lillian maintained a surprising off-again, on-again friendship—and Helma suspected, from her mother's blushes and coyness, more. It was currently off, but that could change in a flash; it had before. "We've been alone too long to give in," Helma's mother liked to say, "and alone too long to give up."

"She's upset by the stolen items and the entire incident, but she's fine. How did you hear about it so quickly? I just came from her apartment."

"At the gym. One of the lifters caught it on his police scanner, and aye, men like to spread a story, too, no offense to you women. He said your mother and aunt wrestled down a killer—a street ruffian—and threw him out the window." He slapped his hands together in a *Splat!* motion. "Is it true?"

"The details are unclear," Helma explained. "It appears a burglar entered the apartment while Aunt Em was napping. She woke up and startled him, and he fell through the window, probably unbalanced by the television in his arms."

"That wee lady scared him? You aren't saying she *pushed* him?" TNT shook his head and his blue eyes probed Helma's as if he could read there what she wasn't saying. "No, I can't believe *that*."

"The excitement is too fresh in Aunt Em's mind right now. She'll recall the details later, when she's able to relax," Helma said.

He nodded. Aunt Em's fuzziness wasn't news. "Then Lil's fine?"

"She is. Why don't you phone her?"

"Ah, I'm on her shite list," he said ruefully in one of his Irishisms. He removed the towel from his neck and wiped his face as if it were dotted with sweat.

"She's forgotten that in all the excitement, I'm sure."

"Do you think?" TNT flexed his shoulders and pulled in his stomach, his face rawly hopeful.

"I do," Helma had no doubt her mother would welcome one more chance to relate the story, managing to squeeze herself a little more into the action.

"Did you see the body?"

Helma nodded. "I didn't recognize him. He had a tattoo." She couldn't help glancing at her own left forearm where the man's crude tattoo had been located.

"What was it? Blokes with tattoos work out at the gym all the time. I may have seen it." His hands raised into fists, sparring with the air.

She described the red heart with its smudged center that might have once held a name or initials.

TNT shook his head. "Not familiar. Might be from out of town, Seattle maybe. Who'd be arse enough to rob gentle ladies in an apartment building?" He raised his hands to the gray sky. "And in the light of the day, too?"

He walked up the stairs to the third floor at Helma's side, muttering, "Got what he deserved."

"You're limping," she noticed.

"Ah, it's nothing. The hips aren't as young as the rest of me anymore."

"You could take the elevator." She nodded toward the elevator that groaned its way from the ground to the third floor, which Helma had never entered, not even when she'd lugged her first box of linens up the steps over twenty years earlier.

"Not a chance. Today's a long day, that's all. My da would say the hitch in my giddy-up meant there's a seventy per cent chance of rain." He shrugged. "But here there's always a seventy per cent chance of rain. What did the blasted thief pinch besides the TV?"

A seagull flapped over the building calling stridently as it headed for the bay. Other gulls joined the call.

"Some jewelry, a few small items. I'm taking Mother and Aunt Em to the police station in the morning to identify and retrieve them."

"Did your mother see the dead man? Was it too much for her?" He inquired cautiously, with a delicacy toward her mother that Helma had never heard in her own father's voice.

She thought again about her conversation with Ruth regarding her mother and Aunt Em's unsurprised acceptance of the robber's death, how swiftly the tragedy had become done-is-done. "She'll want to tell you about it."

He nodded, and at the door to his apartment, smartly saluted her. "And my best wishes to you on your engagement." His blue eyes twinkled. "Our chief is a lucky man."

"How did —" Helma began, and stopped. "Thank you." She'd hoped to keep her engagement private until she'd grown accustomed to the idea herself, but that hope had evaporated. There were no secrets.

Helma took note of Boy Cat Zukas sitting on her balcony railing, staring at his reflection in the sliding glass door that led into her apartment. She paused to scan her rooms to be sure that, yes, her belongings and furnishings were exactly as she'd left them, then she crossed the living room, removed the security stick, and slid open the door.

From two balconies down, apartment 3-D, Jaynie Lynn, who'd informed Helma a week earlier that she'd legally changed her surname from Sanders to Mountain Girl, Yoo-hooed to Helma.

She sat in the lotus position on a plastic lawn chair, wearing a down vest and what looked like pajama bottoms, her long brown hair braided into a coil on top of her head.

Jaynie Lynn's business card, which she'd pinned in various public locations, including on the library's bulletin board and over the Bayside Arms mailboxes, announced she was a "multitasking coach."

Helma waved and waited in her open door for Boy Cat Zukas to enter her apartment.

The cat didn't stir a whisker, but only continued staring as if Helma had turned invisible. She was not in the habit of speaking to animals, so she re-closed the door. By the time she'd switched her brown loafers for a black pair, Boy Cat Zukas was hunkered beside the door yowling to be let in. She could hear him through the glass.

Neither was Helma Zukas a woman to punish animals, but she did fill the bowl beside his wicker bed with dry food and rinse his water dish—*before* she opened the door.

Following her belated shower, she phoned her mother as she watched a pallid sunset. "Is the window repaired?" she asked after her mother's breathless hello. Voices bubbled in the background, women's voices.

"Good as new. Sally and Katherine are here. They brought us dinner. Who could cook after all this excitement? Chicken a la King. Isn't that nice?"

"Very thoughtful. Has Aunt Em remembered any other details about the robbery?"

"Nothing new," In an aside, Helma heard her mother say, "It's my daughter. She's engaged to the chief of police," before she returned to Helma. "Em keeps bragging about how she shoved a killer out the window. When are you picking us up so we can get our things from the police?"

"I'll call you from the library as soon as the police inform me what time."

"The library? You're working tomorrow?"

"Of course. It's Monday."

"But Helma, you just got *engaged*."

"I still have to work. Did you make a list of everything that's missing?"

Her voice dropped. "I'm trying to, but Em keeps interrupting. She forgets what's already on the list and tells me again. That old box. She's told me to include the box about ten times, like it's the only thing in the world."

"What's inside it?"

"I don't think anything's inside it."

"Have you ever looked?"

Her mother was silent for a moment. "Of course not," she said indignantly. "It's Em's personal property."

"Is it locked?"

"It must be, because I couldn't get it open." She giggled, "Whoopsie, I guess I did try to take a small peek once. If it's not a solid block, there must be a trick catch — there's no lock or key hole. But you know how that family was: all secrets and magic, thinking they had a main line into knowledge nobody else shared." She sighed. "Proud of it, even."

Helma winced but said it anyway, luring her mother away from dredging up one of the numerous times she'd felt tricked by "that family." "Did you have a good conversation with Wayne this afternoon?"

"Oh." Delight dripped from her voice, Aunt Em's box forgotten. "He just *loved* my idea of a wedding in the park. We could release doves, wouldn't' that be beautiful, soaring into the sky? All white and fluttery. Nobody does rice anymore. Birds eat it and it swells up in their throats and chokes them to death, or something like that, I can't remember, but I know it's not good."

Helma gazed out at the filmy lights of the last boats on Washington Bay trickling into Squabbly Harbor while her mother planned on. She tried not to listen too closely but picked out a phrase here and there: "five-tiered cake, "matching dresses," "bridal registration."

She was brought back by her doorbell ringing and cut into her mother's flow of conversation about ushers' boutonnières. "Someone's at the door, Mother."

"Is it him?"

"I don't know. I haven't answered it yet."

"Go ahead. I'll wait."

"I'll phone you in the morning."

Her mother sighed. "You really should buy a cordless phone like everybody else, dear. You'd have so much more mobility; you wouldn't have to hang up before you identified your company. Don't you agree it would be safer?"

"Tomorrow morning, Mother. Sleep well."

Wayne Gallant stood on Helma's doormat, a smile already on his face. He'd changed into jeans and a blue pullover. "Sorry I didn't phone first. Your line was busy."

"Come in," she invited, opening the door wide.

He nodded and stepped inside. As always, he filled the space of her apartment. It was curious. He was tall but not heavy. It was just that there seemed so much *more* of him than other people.

"Would you like something to drink?" Tea? A glass of wine?"

"No thanks. I can only stay a minute."

Here was the man with whom Helma had agreed to spend the rest of her life, the man she'd eat meals with, attend events by his side, and the man she'd wake up next to every morning. She swallowed and awkwardly sat in her rocker, stopping its wild gyration by planting both her feet firmly on the floor.

"How are you?" he asked. He sat on the sofa and crossed his right leg over his knee. His foot jiggled up and down.

"I'm fine. And you?"

"Fine." Jiggle, jiggle. He looked at her, the corner of his mouth rose. She looked at him. And as if neither could help it, they began to laugh.

"Helma," he said.

"Wayne," she said at the same time. And they laughed again.

"Well, we've done it now, haven't we?" he said.

"My mother certainly believes so."

He rose from the sofa. She rose from the rocker. Later, Helma couldn't recall either of them taking a single step, but there she was, wrapped in his arms, feeling his breath against her hair.

CHAPTER 6

Changing Numbers

The retrieval of the stolen items was set for ten-thirty a.m. at the Bellehaven police station. That allowed Helma to work two hours at the Bellehaven Public Library before she collected Aunt Em and her mother.

She switched on the morning television news in time to catch the newscaster, Gillian Hovel, who always carefully and somewhat defensively pronounced her surname as "Hoe-VEL," finish a story on a woman arrested for changing her baby's diaper while driving, followed by a brief account of the robber's "plunge" from an upper-floor apartment of the Silver Gables. Thankfully, there was no mention of Lillian or Aunt Em by name, only "elderly widows," but it was a perfect segue into a story titled, "Our beloved elderly: prey for thieves and scams."

The *Bellehaven Daily News*, which was late again, and seemingly even thinner than the previous day's edition, carried the story "below the fold," with a photograph of uniformed police in the Silver Gables parking lot gazing upward at the side of the retirement building, toward the invisible broken fourth floor window. The photo's lower edge was cropped at the policemen's waist level, so there was no chance of glimpsing the body. The words: "...as yet unidentified burglar" jumped out at her. Again, Helma noted with relief, no mention of Lillian or Aunt Em.

The mayor had informed the reporter he was "taking a personal interest" in solving the crime, and promised to hold "ongoing conversations with the Bellehaven police," fulfilling his campaign promise for "a safer city for our good citizens."

The day hung silvery, a slight mist over the bay, the air soft with moisture. No rain today, she could feel that, despite the misty-moisty weather, the second best climate next to sunshine. She'd heard TNT call the combination of mist and moisture "mizzle."

As she crossed the drive toward her Buick in the Bayside Arms carports, Walter David was just stepping out from the carport where he kept his Harley-Davidson motorcycle in the space next to Helma's. Three years earlier he'd added a customized seat on the back for Moggy.

"Morning, Helma. Heard the good news?" the portly manager asked. Moggy, his white Persian cat promenaded in front of him, at the end of a pale blue leash.

"I'm not sure," she replied warily.

Walter David nodded fondly toward Moggy. "We're in the Northwest Regional Fancy Cat semi-finals! Now we start working toward the nationals next month."

Helma glanced at the white cat's flat face with its disturbingly vacant eyes. Its fur draped and flowed with each movement. "Congratulations," she said, more fervently than she intended, so grateful was she that the good news had nothing to do with weddings or dead robbers.

Walter David pulled a cat brush from his jacket pocket and twirled it. White hairs clung to the bristles, as fine as dandelion fluff. "I'm going to teach her to hold a statue pose for five minutes. How many cats have you seen do that?"

She thought of Boy Cat Zukas sitting frozen on her deck, waiting gimlet-eyed for small feathered beings to fly within his reach. "On command?" she said. "None."

"You got it." He smiled and hummed as he and Moggy continued toward Walter's apartment.

She unlocked her car as TNT jogged past, his limp still evident. He gave her a thumbs-up and called, "Back on track!" and Helma guessed his phone call had been successful; her mother and TNT were "on" again.

Bellehaven glistened, as if the mist had cleaned the city like a cloth across a dusty bureau. Cars of employees who worked downtown streamed toward parking lots on the edge of the city core, where parking was available without paying. Helma possessed her own hard-won parking space in the small library parking lot and neatly pulled into it, lining up her Buick's hood ornament with the flagpole on the lawn.

The library occupied one side of a square of city services that included the city hall, the courthouse, the police station, and hospital, all within easy reach. "Government in a box," Ruth called it.

The first thing that met her eyes as she entered the staff entrance off the loading dock was a bright pink banner at eye-level, stretched between her cubicle and an old card catalog the staff now used to store silverware, thumbtacks and small— usually frivolous—office supplies.

It was the generic banner, dragged out when there wasn't time to make a new one. CONGRATULATIONS! it read, and taped to a lower corner was a sheet of copy paper with the words HELMA & WAYNE written in red crayon.

"Didn't think that one was ever going to happen," George Melville, the bearded cataloger, said from his desk where he sat with his feet resting on an open desk drawer. "Congratulations."

Before Helma could answer, Eve, the fiction librarian, was hugging her, her eyes moist. "I'm so, so, so, excited," she squealed.

And then Roger, the children's librarian and Roberta the genealogy/history librarian and Harley the social sciences librarian streamed from the staff room, swarming around her, plus the clerks and pages, even Dutch, the ex-soldier who ran the circulation desk. Their voices buzzed and bumped; bodies orbited around her; hands shook hers; she was hugged and patted. She had to get out of there.

"Excuse me," she told them, raising her hands in surrender. "I must make an important phone call. The police..."

Mention of the police only increased the buzz around her. "Your mother..."; "...fell four stories..."; "Any idea who..."

Then George had his hands on Helma's shoulders, steadying her, saying, "Back off, you vultures. All shall be revealed at a later date. Give her six inches of room to breathe, okay?"

Grumbling, they nevertheless obediently moved away. "You okay?" George asked her.

She nodded. "Thank you."

"You'd think nobody around here ever got engaged and had an aunt commit murder on the same day," George said. "The amateurs."

Helma stepped out from under George's hands. "It wasn't murder."

He shrugged, unconcernedly. "Makes a better story."

Gloria "Call me Glory" Shandy bounced into the workroom from the public area, and George grunted before returning to his desk. Whatever had turned his soulful admiration of Glory into avoidance two years earlier still hadn't been explained or altered.

"Oh, Helma," cooed Glory, who, although still the youngest librarian on the staff of the Bellehaven Public Library, hadn't recovered from once being younger than she was now. "Congratulations." She chortled and tugged at the baby blue hair bow that perfectly matched the ruffles on the bodice of her dress. "Oh, that's naughty of me. You're not supposed to congratulate the bride-to-be; you say that to the groom-to-be." She bit her lip and screwed an index finger into her cheek to form a dimple. "But maybe when you're so much older than the usual bride-to-be, congratulations *are* in order." She tipped her head at Helma, her eyelashes batting.

"Thank you," Helma said judiciously, and edged away toward her cubicle.

"I hope you'll be very, very, wonderfully, happy," Glory went on, following Helma. "What a humungous change for you, after all these years alone—I mean, as a single woman." She nodded sagely. "There will be *so* much to get used to. I had an aunt who married late in her life, too, and her marriage barely lasted a month. My mother said she was sorry she'd even bought Aunt Julie a wedding gift."

George's voice wafted across the workroom. "Jealous?"

"Hmmph," Glory sniffed, and finally abandoned Helma, flouncing back toward the public area.

She shouldn't have come to work. She set her bag on her desk, contemplating her options. There was the new printer policy she'd been drafting. On the other hand, she wasn't scheduled for the reference desk that morning, so it wasn't crucial she remain.

A muffled "Mmm," came from the cubicle next to Helma's. Harley Woodworth, whom George called "Hardly Worthit," sat at his desk, separated from Helma by a low bookcase. He sat beneath his full-colored "Dangerous Moles" poster, inspecting his face in a hand-held mirror, tipping his head to one side, then the other. Holding his thumb and forefinger to his chin, he smoothed back the flesh along his long jaws, stretching it until it was taut and shiny. Then he smiled at himself, baring his teeth as if he were examining them for errant food particles.

Harley glanced up and saw Helma watching him. His face flashed red and he dropped his mirror, diving beneath his desk after it.

May Apple Moon's office was visible from Helma's cubicle. The director's door stood open, as was her stated policy, and faint sounds of George Frideric Handel's *"Wassermusik"* drifted from its depths, which signaled she was working on plans for the new library. Ms. Moon played Handel's Water Music each time she tinkered with the new library plans, claiming Handel was a mnemonic, immediately putting her into "the most beneficial and consistently creative mindset," allowing her to "visualize the hopes and dreams of Bellehaven's community of readers."

The staff had heard "*Wassermusik*" every day for months, and Helma doubted if any of them would ever willingly listen to Handel again.

She tipped her head slightly to hear better and recognized "Air," indicating Ms. Moon was deep into the Suite, and therefore, deep into the distraction of the new library's plans

Ms. Moon looked up when Helma tapped lightly on the doorjamb and before the director's face rounded in a beaming smile, a flash of irritation narrowed her eyes. She flicked off Handel. "Helma, Helma, come in." She opened her arms to encompass the entire office, which she'd recently had changed from a verdant green hue to pale blue: "shades of sky and freedom."

Helma remained in the doorway. "I have an urgent family matter to attend to, so I'm requesting the remainder of the morning as leave time."

"Family matter?" Ms. Moon repeated, tapping her mechanical pencil on the border of the much-amended and erased blueprints. "Urgent?"

Ms. Moon's vagaries as she immersed herself in repositioning rooms, altering shelving sites, and fussing over the comparative height of wastebaskets, were at once perplexing to the staff—and a relief: distracting the director was shockingly easy.

The stringent budget for the new library was a constant challenge. "We must have..." was a recurring mantra, and Ms. Moon was apt to lick her lips and whip a calculator from her pocket at the slightest mention of juicier paraphernalia, such as dimmer-switches, self-replacing bathroom tissue rolls, and motion-activated checkout computers.

"Did you come to a decision over the width of the new children's book-return slot?" Helma asked now, and Ms. Moon began shuffling through the spread of blueprints, murmuring and frowning, losing interest in Helma.

"I'll return by one o'clock," Helma said.

"Mm-hmm,"

The staff had taken to informing Dutch of schedule changes. She found him in the public area contemplating the new bestseller display. The display was only four days old and occupied a two-tier table positioned between the check-out desk and the library's main entrance. George had called its location as good as a snare trap hidden in high grass. "They crash into it coming and going," his "they" being the library's patrons.

Multiple copies of current bestsellers covered the table, as artfully arranged as a bookstore. In fact, the table contained more copies of individual titles than most of the dwindling number of bookstores kept in stock.

"This is what they're mad about," Dutch said, more to himself than to Helma.

"Who?"

Dutch turned his thumb-shaped head toward her, frowning. He was a retired military man, one of Ms. Moon's surprise hires, and he'd taken command of the circulation desk with the fervor of General Patton. His was a clerical position, actually, but his military métier had gradually led to all the staff falling under his command. Library pages jumped when he spoke, and didn't even attempt to hide from him in the less-frequented corners of the library. If a librarian dealt with a "behaviorally unpredictable" patron, it was Dutch whom they hoped would loom up behind them.

He ran his hand across his graying brush cut and said in an ominous voice, "You'll find out," and returned to the circulation desk, where he began slamming returned books into even-heighted stacks.

"Wait up!"

Ruth slammed the door of her aging Saab, which she'd parked at an angle too far from the curb in the library's fifteen-minute zone. Her car was curiously colorless, shaped like a cartoon car.

Helma removed her key from the driver's door of her Buick. She did not shout in public, so she waited until Ruth strode within speaking distance before she said, "I thought you were painting today." Ruth wore a man's gray sweatshirt over the same blue clothes she'd worn the day before.

"Hah. Weren't you listening to me? There is no talent in these fingers. Nada." Ruth shook her hands and let them drop as if they were boneless. "Maybe never again. I've degenerated into painting little birds sitting on flowers in front of windmills."

Since Helma had rarely known Ruth to paint anything recognizable, she considered Ruth's words an exaggerated bid for attention. "There's really no reason for you to accompany us to the police station."

"It'll be more interesting than cleaning paintbrushes. And maybe I can find a new cop for my collection. Unlock the passenger door, will you?"

The air around Ruth was charged with discontent, like a day in the Midwest when lightning flashed in the distance—weather coming—times when it was safest to be as far from Ruth as possible.

"Have you tried switching mediums?" Helma tried. "Instead of oils, pastels?"

"C'mon," Ruth said, making key-turning motions with her hand. "Let me in."

"Ruth…"

"I can tuck your Aunt Em in and out of the car, free you up to deal with your mother."

"Mother can help Aunt Em."

"Yeah. I know what your mother is on fire to discuss. And it doesn't have anything to do with murder and robbery, either." Ruth made "Dum-dum-de-dum" sounds to the tune of Wagner's *Bridal Chorus*. "I'll distract her for you."

Helma reconsidered. Ruth's presence *did* have the effect of dampening Lillian's enthusiasm. "Wouldn't you like to have *nice* friends, Helma?" her mother had asked the first time Helma brought Ruth home from school in fourth grade.

Lillian and Aunt Em sat side by side on a wooden bench in front of the Silver Gables. They waved in unison as Helma steered her car into the circular drive. Aunt Em's green polyester pantsuit was topped by a black felt hat that appeared to have originated in the 1940s. She leaned heavily on her cane to stand. Helma's mother wore a new blue dress and low pumps.

"Very mother-of-the-bride-ish," Ruth commented as Helma stopped the car.

"You ride up front with Helma," Ruth told Aunt Em as she opened her door and stepped out. "Lillian and I will sit in back."

"What a nice girl you are," Aunt Em said as Ruth helped her fasten her seatbelt.

"She's hardly a girl." Lillian gave an audible sniff.

"Next to me she is," Aunt Em countered. "Maybe next to you, too."

"Do you have your list of stolen items?" Helma asked when they were finally all buckled and settled inside, before she pulled away from the curb.

"Of course I have it," Lillian said, and Helma heard the pat-pat-pat of her mother tapping her purse.

"Did you write my *Stelmužė* box on the list?" Aunt Em asked.

"Yes, Em," Lillian assured her, adding in a lower voice, "Only about fifty times."

"That must be for you, Aunt Em," Helma said as she stopped in front of the police station. Camella, the policewoman who'd questioned Lillian and Aunt Em after the robbery, stood at the curb with one hand on the back of a wheelchair, the other holding an umbrella.

Camella wasn't wearing her policewoman's uniform, but a black skirt and red sweater, the only evidence of her status the badge at her waist.

"She didn't need to do that," Aunt Em protested, but she didn't decline.

"Good morning, ladies," Camella greeted them. She smiled at Aunt Em, her eyes drifting past Helma without pausing.

They helped Aunt Em into the chair and Camella wheeled her ahead, leading them up the sidewalk and into the station. Helma noted the extra solicitous way the policewoman treated Aunt Em, as if her sole aspiration was to soothe away any discomfort of Aunt Em's, even pausing to ask Aunt Em if she'd like a blanket over her lap.

Aunt Em rejected the offer. "It will make wrinkles."

The solicitousness was more than just because Aunt Em was aged and frail. But why? The only reason for Aunt Em and Lillian's appearance was to identify and repossess their stolen items.

Had there been another development? Something to do with the robber's death?

Camella escorted them to a large, bright office painted a warm yellow. Cloth dolls, one of them an anatomically correct boy, sat on a shelf in the corner. Bright cushions and comfortable chairs—it was a room used to question children, to alleviate the fear from witnessing or being part of a terrifying situation.

"Here we are," Camella said cheerfully, helping Aunt Em from the wheelchair into an overstuffed chair.

Helma glanced at Ruth and saw the frown on her face. She was thinking the same thing—more was going on here than the retrieval of a few trinkets.

Wayne Gallant entered the room and Lillian beamed, first bestowing a wide smile on him, then more of an encouraging smile on Helma, as if she were adding a wordless message for Helma to "be nice." He returned Lillian's smile, but it was a professional smile, all business.

Even accounting for their personal association, it was curious that the chief of police was following up on a burglary. But, there *had* been a death, and unnatural deaths weren't that common in Bellehaven. And, she reminded herself, the mayor's "personal interest" in solving the case had likely escalated to "personal pressure."

Detective Carter Houston followed behind the chief, carrying a white cardboard box.

"Hey, look," Ruth announced. "It's Detective Carter,"

Carter Houston flinched but only replied, "Good morning," glancing around the room to include them all.

The detective, who did, as Aunt Em claimed, resemble a plastic blow-up toy that children punched but that jumped right back up again, had fallen victim to Ruth years ago, from the first moment he'd stepped into her presence. His invisible sense of humor was a beacon to Ruth, who couldn't help herself: she pricked and poked and bedeviled him, trying—Helma suspected—to find the spot that would collapse him at last like a popped balloon so she could dust off her hands and walk away victorious. So far, she'd been unsuccessful, which only encouraged her all the more.

"Are our things in there?" Lillian asked, pointing to Carter's box. "My ring?"

"And my *Stelmužė* box," Aunt Em added. "Did you put my box on the list, Lillian?"

"The chief has demoted you to working in evidence now, Carter?" Ruth asked.

Carter normally managed the grimmest investigations: murder, high-level bribery or million-dollar drug cases—not stolen property.

Carter set the box in the middle of the table, the lid still on it and a printed bar code stamped on the top with yesterday's date scribbled in ballpoint. He handed a full-sized sheet of paper to Wayne. Aunt Em eagerly leaned forward.

"Here's *our* list." Lillian removed a folded sheet of paper from her purse and also gave it to Wayne. "I printed it off my computer. Every missing piece is on it. We checked all our nooks and crannies, just like you told us. I'm also missing a silver serving spoon, but I think Em left it at one of her pot lucks." Aunt Em silently shook her head, glancing at the ceiling.

Wayne held the two lists in front of him, peering from one to the other, his expression only evincing concentration. Helma recognized the stillness on his face. He was puzzled. They all sat silently, watching and waiting.

He finally nodded to Carter who removed the lid from the cardboard box. None of them could help it; they leaned forward to peer inside, and Helma remembered an old children's book her nephews had loved with an illustration of a band of pirates rearing back in horror from a treasure chest as bats and beasts foamed out of it in an unexpected rush.

"But..." Lillian said.

"My *Stelmužė* box," Aunt Em moaned.

The cardboard box contained a broken ceramic angel with gilded hem and wings, four silver iced tea spoons, the VFW plaque, and one pair of pearl earrings Helma recognized as her father's twenty-fifth anniversary present to her mother. Lillian reached into the box and pushed the contents from one side of the box to the other, coming up with her opal ring, but nothing more.

'Is that everything?" Helma asked.

"My wedding band." Lillian sounded as mournful as Aunt Em. "Where is it?"

Tears slid from Aunt Em's eyes and Camella laid a hand on her shoulder, murmuring words Helma couldn't hear.

"Somebody robbed the robber?" Ruth asked. "When? While he was stretched out dead on the pavement?"

"We're talking to nearby businesses and residents today," Wayne told them. "Several people phoned 9-1-1 after they heard the window break or saw the body. The police response was fast."

"But a bystander saw an opportunity and was faster," Helma guessed.

"That's a possibility."

"Did you ID the dead guy yet?" Ruth asked, and the image of the still body on the pavement with its arc of blood appeared in Helma's mind before she had time to banish it.

Wayne nodded and opened the manila folder he'd carried in with him. "Steven Block," he read. "Called 'Chip Block.'"

"As in Chip off the old Block?" Helma asked.

He nodded. "Does the name mean anything to any of you?"

They all shook their heads.

"Prior burglary convictions:" the chief went on, "breaking and entering, minor theft. He's from Seattle, drifted around the state, no current address."

"What was Steven Block's connection to the Silver Gables?" Helma asked. "Did he have a relative living in one of the apartments? Was he a former employee?"

He closed the folder and rested his hands on top of it. "No connections that we've discovered so far."

"I *know* my list is right," Helma's mother appealed to Carter. "Em and I went through the apartment more than once, I assure you. We were very careful."

"What about the security cameras?" Helma asked.

The chief's mouth thinned to a tight line. "We're still looking," he said, and Helma knew the cameras had truly been broken, just as the manager had claimed. It was a good reason for Lillian and Aunt Em to look for another place to live. But maybe not; wasn't it true that nothing caused security to become more vigilant than a breach in that security? The same as if a person who left his door unlocked came home and discovered his house ransacked, probably never left his door unlocked again.

Aunt Em still gazed forlornly into the white box. "My *Stelmužė* box," she said again. Then she looked up and asked in a quiet voice, "Do you think the other robber has it?"

CHAPTER 7

The Rule of Two

Conversation skittered to a halt and all eyes turned to Aunt Em.

"The other robber?" Wayne Gallant asked gently, without emphasis, as if he were merely continuing a conversation he and Aunt Em had been exclusively engaged in.

"*Taip*. He didn't go out the window like the one you found."

Helma's mother broke the mood by leaning toward Aunt Em and stridently accusing, "You never said there were *two* robbers, Em. What other robber?"

"I don't know his name," Aunt Em retorted sharply. Her chin rose.

Wayne knelt in front of Aunt Em and smiled. She returned his smile and Helma caught the tiny glint in her eye. Nearly ninety or not, it was the same glint Helma had glimpsed in Aunt Em's eyes when she'd once found her sitting alone in the weight room of the Silver Gables watching the men sweat and strain over heavy weights. "Then were there *two* robbers?" Wayne asked. "Or three?"

"Just two," she replied with certainty.

"Can you tell me what the other robber looked like?"

She gave an exaggerated shrug, and this time Helma recognized a familiar movement identical to her father's, that expressive overemphasized raise of the shoulders accompanied by wrinkled forehead, pursed mouth, wide eyes, and open hands.

"Like anybody," Aunt Em said. "Normal. A little..." She looked upward.

"Glasses?" Camella questioned.

"Bald?" Lillian asked

"Tall?" Helma tried. "Was the man tall?"

Aunt Em nodded. "Helma is right. Tall, like Ruthie." She smiled at Ruth who gave her a thumbs-up sign. "One burglar went out the window, one went out the door."

"Do you remember any words they said to each other?" Wayne asked her.

"Maybe." She frowned. Her hands fluttered. "Ah, this old age. It tricks you."

Wayne patted her arm and rose. "Don't even think about it now. If you do remember, tell Lillian or Helma, all right?"

"I can do that."

"I'll be right back." Wayne beckoned for Camella and Carter to follow him out of the room.

The women sat digesting this startling new information. *Two* robbers? Helma bit her lips together to keep from peppering Aunt Em with questions that would only confuse her more. Even Aunt Em was cruelly aware of her slipping memory, the occasions when she'd be firmly in the present and yet, somehow, yesterday or last week, or even fifty years past would bleed into Now, as if time had stopped being linear and become an eddy that swirled back on itself.

"Tell me why you call it your *Stelmužė* box," Helma asked.

"There is an oak tree as old as God," she told Helma, both hands resting on the table and cupping an invisible box. "The wood came from that tree."

Ruth tapped her forehead. "Please don't tell me this is one of those pieces of the 'one true cross' relics."

"Of course not. This is real."

"He took *my* ring, too." Lillian leaned between Helma and Aunt Em. "Don't forget that."

"What kind of doll is that?" Aunt Em suddenly asked, pointing to the anatomically correct boy doll.

"You shouldn't look at it," Lillian said.

"But *you* can? Just because I don't have a man, and you and that old boxer are..."

"Hush, Emily," Lillian ordered in a loud whisper. Aunt Em snorted and Ruth cast a speculative glance at Lillian, tipping her head.

"That old boxer, that DDT," Aunt Em said.

"It's TNT," Lillian said stiffly.

"TNT," Aunt Em repeated. "Ah, well. He is not as good as my brother, but he's probably a good enough man for you."

Lillian's eyes widened. She smiled and touched her hair. "Do you really think so?"

"Maybe," Aunt Em conceded.

Wayne and Carter Houston returned to the room and Lillian took advantage of the diversion of their entrance to throw a gaily colored clown strategically over the boy doll.

"Carter is our best detective," Wayne said, and Ruth made little clapping motions without sound.

Carter brushed at an invisible spot on his sharply pressed suit coat sleeve. Helma had never seen Carter Houston wearing anything except black suits and black shoes, even on the rare instances she'd glimpsed him outside of police work.

"He'll be conducting the investigation into the burglary and death," Wayne continued, "so you'll be seeing him frequently. I know you'll cooperate with him."

Helma thought of the humorless by-the-rules detective questioning Aunt Em and interjected, "I'd like to be present whenever my mother or Aunt Em are questioned."

"Any problem with that, Carter?" Wayne asked.

"Not at the moment," Carter answered with a touch of fussiness.

"Am I wanted for murder?" Aunt Em asked. A hint of excitement raised her voice.

"Definitely not," Wayne assured her.

"If there were two robbers," Helma said, "the other robber likely has my mother's ring and Aunt Em's box. Also," she continued, "this may explain the death: a disagreement between thieves, which ended in the identified burglar's death."

"That's efficient," Ruth added. "The bad eliminating the bad. I like it. Just think how a chain reaction like that could benefit the world. Could put you out of business, Carter."

"No fear of that, Miss Winthrop," Carter told Ruth, then snapped his mouth closed as if he'd embarrassed himself by responding. The tips of his ears pinked.

Aunt Em gazed up at Carter. "Will you find my *Stelmužė* box for me?" She made carving motions with her hands.

Carter's voice softened. He almost smiled at Aunt Em. "We'll try, ma'am. Do you have a photograph of it?"

"I had the box; I didn't need a photo." She brightened. "But Ruth can draw it. I'll talk it to her and she'll draw it and we'll give it to you. Can you do it, Ruthie?"

"Together, you and I will make a picture that's better than a photo."

"I thought so," Aunt Em said.

"Ma'am," Carter asked Aunt Em. "Can you explain what that means: a stil...?" He closed his lips as if unwilling to declare his ignorance with any further mispronunciations.

"*Stelmužė* is a village in Liet...Lithuania." She pronounced it "Lit-wania." "The wood came from a tree near there and my Papa carved it."

"Did you keep jewelry or anything valuable inside the box?"

Aunt Em shook her head. "No. Nothing. My Papa made it for me in Lithuania."

A cell phone suddenly rang, and in that curious way that made it impossible to tell the origin of a cell phone ring, Ruth, the two policemen, and Lillian all scrambled to find their phones.

Lillian squinted at hers, smiled, poked a button and abruptly stood, sending her chair rocking, the phone in her hand. "This is a very important phone call," she announced briskly. "You have our lists. I'll look for photos of my missing jewelry, too."

With her free hand she reached into the white box and scooped up the broken angel and silver teaspoons. "I'll take these and you drive us home, Helma." She smiled at Wayne Gallant. "Helma and I have a year's worth of planning to do."

"One more question," Carter Houston said, holding up his hand.

"Later, later," Lillian told him, heading for the door. "Call Helma and we'll talk soon," sounding as if on some convenient day in the distant future she and the detective might have lunch.

"*I* want to hear his question," Aunt Em said stubbornly, not moving a muscle.

Lillian shook her head, held up her cell phone as explanation, and left the room

"Names," Carter said. "Do you remember hearing either burglar call the other one by a name?"

Aunt Em thought, the ridges of wrinkles on her forehead folding one into another. "Not a real name like Carter or Ruth or Lillian, but 'Stupid,' like 'What are you doing, stupid?' or 'Why did you do that, idiot?' Like that." Again, she raised her shoulders in that exaggerated shrug. "Not good boys."

"Did they fight?" Carter made fisticuff motions and Ruth grinned at him.

"Not with me," Aunt Em said.

"With each other?" He squinted, his voice unusually gentle. "Pushing each other?"

"And out the window, you mean?" Aunt Em asked. Her eyes suddenly filled with tears. "I can't remember," she told him in a small voice, winding her arthritic hands together.

Helma stood and laid her hand on Aunt Em's shoulder. "She's answered all your questions that she can. We're ready to leave now." She turned to Camella. "If my aunt could use the wheelchair again?"

"Of course," Camella agreed in her pleasant voice, but Helma caught the hot gleam as Camella's eyes caught hers and slid away.

At the Silver Gables, Ruth jumped out and grabbed one of the wheelchairs that always lined the foyer. "If the police can do it, we can, too," she told Aunt Em. "Hop in."

Helma left Lillian, Ruth, and Aunt Em waiting in front of the elevator doors, Lillian already regaling a waiting blonde woman with the breathy tale of "assisting my future son-in-law, the chief of police," while Helma took the stairs, arriving at the fourth floor before she heard the ding of the arriving elevator.

A blue plastic vase of mixed flowers sat in front of the apartment door. "They're for you," Helma told Aunt Em as she picked up the vase and read the card.

"It's not my birthday."

"An admirer, Em," Ruth said.

"Are you sure they're for Em?" Lillian asked. "Let me see the card."

"That's what the card says," Helma told her, and Aunt Em said, "You read it for me, Wilhelmina."

"Shall we take it inside first?"

"Now. I might not want that bouquet when I know who sent it."

Helma opened the florist's card and read aloud, "We're sorry to hear of your robbery." She skipped reading the list of eight Lithuanian names, and went right to "From your Lithuanian Club."

Aunt Em nodded. "Will I miss Rimas's funeral?"

"Oh, Em." Lillian patted Aunt Em's shoulder. "That was yesterday. You forgot with all our excitement."

"I forget *without* excitement," Aunt Em told her sadly.

"Big deal." Ruth pushed the wheelchair into the apartment. "I have tons of things I wish I could forget."

"I'm sure," Lillian said, and then at Helma's glance, hastily added, "I mean, we all do."

"I'm sure," Ruth responded.

Helma set the vase in her mother's sink and rearranged the flowers so the reds and blues were more balanced, and as she positioned the vase in the middle of the dining room table, the phone rang.

"Answer that, will you, Helma?" her mother, who was untangling Aunt Em from her coat, asked. "If it's for me, I'll take it to my bedroom." She giggled.

Helma was greeted by a barrage of Lithuanian in a woman's voice. Her own Lithuanian was limited to the basics: hello, goodbye, how are you. "Excuse me," she interrupted the flow. "May I help you?"

The woman made clucking sounds and switched to unaccented English. "I'm sorry. I thought you were Emily. You sound like her."

She did? "No. Who's calling, please?"

"Anna Klimas. When Em wasn't at Rimas's funeral, I was worried. But then we heard she was robbed." Her voice dropped to a whisper, "And the robber's dead. Poor Em — a shock like that — you never know, do you? Oh, my. We thought flowers might cheer her up. Did she get them? You don't know sometimes. Things happen."

Helma unconsciously glanced at the bouquet. "The flowers arrived a while ago—a very attractive bouquet of mixed blooms." She didn't mention the disarrangement of colors. Then she glanced at Aunt Em, whose eyes were closed. "My aunt is resting."

"What was stolen? Anything valuable?"

"May I ask Aunt Em to call you back?"

Anna Klimas sighed. "When she's up to it. I'm going to take a little nap myself. I've had a very busy day."

Then Helma recognized the name, Klimas. "Was Rimas your husband? Aunt Em felt badly about missing the funeral."

"My brother. He was a sick man for years."

"I'm sorry."

"He was ready to die," Anna Klimas said matter-of-factly. "And we gave him a proper Lugan send-off."

Lugan was a slang term so detrimental only Lithuanians could use it to refer to themselves, it being a fighting word if a non-Lithuanian said it: In high school, there'd been a near-riot when the Polish Manistee boys taunted the taller Scoop River boys on the basketball court.

"I'll ask Aunt Em to call you," Helma repeated, and made her goodbyes.

"Who was that?" Lillian asked as Helma jotted down the woman's name and phone number on the purple notepad beside the phone.

"Anna Klimas, a friend of Aunt Em's."

"Friend," Helma's mother sniffed. "She's a nosy one. Did she try to squeeze the robbery details out of you?"

"Mother, her brother just died and Aunt Em's club was thoughtful enough to send her flowers. She was confirming they'd arrived."

"As a means of entry." Helma's mother was back to reading mysteries again. Lillian turned to Aunt Em. "Did you take your pills, Em?"

Without opening her eyes, Aunt Em waved a hand toward the dining room table. "Don't ask me. Check your machine."

Lillian straightened, a slight but eager smile on her face, and bustled to her computer where it still sat open on the table. She clicked the mouse and tut-tutted, looking through the bottom of her eyes at the screen, reached for her glasses, clicked some more, and announced, "Almost time. I'll get them ready."

The second she rose, Ruth moved to the computer as if she were stalking game. She squinted, then shook her head in wonder and beckoned for Helma to join her.

"You ever see anything like this before?"

The screen in front of them held a spreadsheet titled, "Emily." On it were listed dates and times and types of medication, with spaces for symptoms and "food intake."

"Isn't that the cleverest thing?" Lillian asked as she returned from the kitchen carrying a glass of water and a book-sized plastic pill box marked with the days of the week in giant letters, four compartments for each day. "I designed it myself."

But before Helma could get a really good look at the spreadsheet and decipher the entries, Lillian's hand shot between her and Ruth and tapped the mouse, blinking the screen to darkness.

"I wish there'd been computers when you were a baby," Lillian said. "Just think of all the information I could have kept."

"A veritable treasure trove," Ruth agreed, nodding her head too eagerly. "Helma's teething habits, potty training records. All her little throw-ups."

"Well," Lillian said defensively, casting Ruth a sidelong glance. "Em's doctor loves it. He can see at a glance what's going on. Make predictions for—"

"—when I will die?" Aunt Em finished.

"Don't talk like that, Em." Lillian said briskly as she poured the pills onto a small saucer and set the glass of water in front of Aunt Em.

"Do you think your mother's started a wedding file on her computer for you?" Ruth asked in a low voice.

"Please don't suggest it," Helma warned her in an equally low voice, suspecting her mother had already done exactly that.

"Helma, will you take me to the Lithuanian Club?" Aunt Em asked.

"Of course, whenever you like."

"Do I need my jacket?" Two pills still waited on the saucer.

"You want to go *now*?" Lillian asked as she slid the saucer closer to Aunt Em's hand. "You're too tired."

"I'm not so tired. I want to thank them for the flowers." Helma could see Aunt Em's eyes closing on their own accord.

"Write them a note, Em," Lillian said. "I'll put it in the mailbox at the desk for you, and they'll get it tomorrow."

"I could deliver a card to the club for you, Aunt Em," Helma offered. "I'll drop it off on the way home."

"I have boxes of notecards," Lillian told Aunt Em, heading for her bedroom.

"Not your cards with bears riding bicycles," Aunt Em called after her. "Something nice."

CHAPTER 8

Clubs on Deck

Holding a ballpoint pen like a dagger, Aunt Em laboriously wrote her thank you on a notecard decorated with sunflowers, and asked Helma to insert it into the envelope. "My hands are too clumsy."

"I can do it," Helma's mother interrupted, holding out her hand. "I'm standing right here."

Aunt Em pulled the envelope close. "You want to read it to tell me what I wrote wrong. Helma can do it. Lick the envelope closed, Wilhelmina. Tight."

Lillian stepped away, mumbling. Helma didn't lick envelopes. She ran water over her finger at the kitchen faucet and moistened the envelope's flap before she sealed in the card and tucked it in her purse.

"I'll phone you as soon as I hear from Carter Houston or the chief," she assured her mother and aunt one more time.

"Slide the card into the mailbox slot in the door of my club," Aunt Em reminded Helma again as the door closed.

"You know where this place is?" Ruth asked. Her voice echoed against the concrete walls of the stairwell.

Helma nodded. "They're leasing the old Boy Scout building."

"For once-a-month meetings they leased a whole building? How many members?"

"Fifteen to twenty."

"Must pay hefty dues." Ruth frowned. "Or did they come up with a wealthy benefactor?"

Helma hadn't thought of the cost before. It had to be expensive. "I don't know," she admitted, resolving to find out.

The one-story building sat on a busy street surrounded by houses from the 1940s and 1950s that were being renovated into insurance offices and hair salons, an architectural mish-mash. The street had been patched with so many lines of tar they looked like graffiti.

She pulled into the gravel lot and parked her Buick straight in as if there were marked parking spaces. A single blue van sat crookedly near the building's front door. Lights were on inside, but there were no figures visible through the tall windows.

"I'll just drop this in the mail slot like Aunt Em asked," Helma told Ruth, who was already opening her door. "I'll be right back."

"Nah, I want to look around," Ruth said, slamming the passenger door overloud. She followed on Helma's heels to the building's front door, humming under her breath. A forlorn badge-shape of lighter paint over the door was all that remained of the Boy Scouts' tenancy.

There was no mail slot in the scabbily-painted door. Helma wondered if Aunt Em had misremembered, recalling instead some door that had existed fifty years earlier in Michigan, or seventy years ago in Chicago.

Ruth rattled the door. "Hey, it's open." She turned the doorknob and stepped inside.

Helma finally found a slot hidden by bushes in the wall to the right of the door—nailed over long ago by a strip of plywood that was now colorless and degraded. She reluctantly followed Ruth into the Lithuanian Club.

The pale green vestibule, holding a battered desk, was empty. Papers sat on the desktop. First, Helma lifted an open *Bellehaven Daily News*, searching for a bell to ring. Not finding one, she spoke in a certainly conversational, but attention-getting voice, "Hello?"

When no one answered, Ruth called out in her big voice. "Hey! Anybody here? You've got company."

Beyond the vestibule a doorway stood open to a meeting room with one wall painted Boy Scout khaki, a linoleum floor, folding chairs, a long folding table with more chairs, and tables stacked against the walls. American and Lithuanian flags hung limply on stands in the front of the room, both flagpoles topped by bronze eagles.

"Quick," Ruth said, turning in a circle. "Tell me what country I'm in."

Helma knew exactly what she meant. The single room was reminiscent of the already-in-decay town halls and Lithuanian and German halls she remembered as a child in Michigan.

A small and rudimentary kitchen with a pass-through window stood off to one side, where in her memory the women usually ended up preparing food and discussing who did what and to whom.

"Throw in an accordion and too much booze and we've got a memory in the making," Ruth said, leaning across the pass-through counter.

"I'll leave Aunt Em's card on the desk." Helma glanced down at the envelope. Aunt Em had written in a shaky hand, "To My Kind Friends." And even though it hadn't been intended for the post office, she'd carefully written her full return address in the upper left corner.

Ruth strolled along a line of framed photos on the longest wall, frowning at the faces. "You guys all kind of look alike," she commented. "Cheekbones, widow's peaks, something funny around the eyes."

Helma glanced at the photos: mostly elderly men, the departed or aging members of the club, a few photos of sparsely attended dinners, and a scene of women wearing traditional dress, lined across a stage. One black-and-white photograph of Lithuania's famous Hill of Crosses, and another of the equally famous Trakai Castle on its tiny island in the middle of Lake Galvé.

She paused in front of a photograph of Aunt Em taken at least forty years earlier: bold-eyed, head erect, gazing directly into the camera lens. Taken before Helma had learned all the secrets hidden behind those eyes.

"*Labas*, hello," sang out a woman's voice. Helma looked up to see a fair-haired woman enter the vestibule carrying a Starbuck's paper cup. "I'm sorry. I just stepped out for a coffee. I'm the clean-up team, but can I help you?" She was tall and slender, in her late forties, with a sense of "movement" about her.

Before either Helma or Ruth could answer, the door banged open and a tall young man stepped inside carrying an envelope. "Here they are," he said, giving the envelope to the woman. "Dad just had them printed."

"Thank you, dear. Give him my love."

"Sure." He nodded, his glance sweeping over all three women.

"Wait just a second," she told him. "I'd better check them first." She spread three eight-by-ten photos on the desk, murmuring, "Mm, mmm" over them.

The man pulled out a cell phone, thumbing the tiny keyboard while he waited, oblivious to them. Ruth sidled closer to him as if he were magnetized and she a steel ball, as she always did in the presence of a tall man, basking in their comparative height, an expression of contentment lighting her face.

The woman looked up and said, "These are good, I mean, the photographs, of course, their quality. I'm sorry about your grandfather, Tony. I know how close you were to him. He -"

"Yeah," the young man cut her off, slipped his phone in his pants pocket, nodded again, and left. The door closed with a thud behind him.

"He's broken hearted," the fair-haired woman commented, peering at the closed front door.

"Look at these, would you?" Ruth leaned over the desk and touched the edge of one of the photos. "What are they, family portraits?"

All three photos depicted the same elderly man lying in a white, satin-lined casket, his hands folded together over his black-suited chest: one alone, the second with an elderly woman standing at the end of the casket and gazing down at him, her own hands clasped in unconscious imitation. The last photo included five other people solemnly regarding the deceased man, obviously family by the similarly hawked noses, high cheekbones, and even apparent in photographs, considerable height.

"For your Dead Lithuanians scrapbook?" Ruth asked.

Instead of being offended, the woman laughed. "You're not far wrong. They're for the club. Little bit ghoulish, aren't they? I'm Dalia Stone. Did you know Rimas?" She tapped the photo of the man in his casket.

Helma shook her head. "My Aunt Em did. She had planned to attend the funeral." She held up the card. "She asked me to drop this by, thanking you for the flowers."

"You're Emily's niece? The flowers were all right? We were sorry to hear about..." she hesitated, trying to put a name to the robbery and death. "...the accident," she ended, shrugging as if she knew that inadequately expressed the event. "Have the police found her heirlooms yet?"

"Not yet."

"Oh, but the very best boys in blue are hot on it," Ruth added.

"Why would they rob Emily, I wonder. Maybe it's a gang targeting old people."

"Then they should target *rich* old people," Ruth said.

"Are you related to Rimas?" Helma asked Dalia, who lined the three photos across the desk, studying each one.

"No, no." She pointed to the photo with the elderly woman. "This is Anna, his sister." Then the group photo. "And this is Rimas's daughter, and this is his son and family. Some came from here for the funeral, some from Back East."

"Back East" was a term Bellehavenites used to describe all land that existed from the other side of the Cascades to the Atlantic Ocean.

Dalia's finger hovered over one of the young men in the family photo. "That's Tony, who just dropped off the pictures, Rimas's grandson. They were close. Here's his granddaughter Pamela from Massachusetts—she's a cutie. And her kids are just as cute. Everybody's scattered these days, aren't they?" She squinted at Helma. "But your aunt is here with her family – that's nice. Have you thought of joining the club with Emily?"

"Not really. I'm a generation removed."

"Me, too," Dalia told her. "But here I am, finding my roots and all that. Nice people. And it's good way to practice my Lithuanian. My *Lietuvishkai*."

"I've never visited Lithuania," Helma told her.

"Ah, it's a good place, especially since independence. A little..." She looked up at Ruth and said curiously, "*You'd* like it."

As they left the Lithuanian club, Dalia patted Helma's hand as if she were comforting her. "Everybody's so happy Emily wasn't hurt. And if anything comes of the ...other, well, we all know it was self-defense."

After she dropped off Ruth, who was muttering, "They're all tall. *I'm* the tall one, not you; I still suspect we were switched at birth." Helma returned to the library. Turning the corner of Center Street, she was shocked to see a line of people slowly circling on the sidewalk in front of the library's main entrance, carrying placards. A strike? She hadn't heard any rumblings of discontent from the staff, wasn't aware of any local groups upset over library books or programs.

She slowed, recognizing a local mystery author, and tried to read their signs, but only caught the faintly printed word "Rights" before a car behind her honked and she drove on. Whatever group he represented, they hadn't researched the impact of proper print and font sizes for easy reading from distances.

"Who's picketing the library?" she asked George Melville, the first librarian she met on entering the library workroom. He carried a coffee cup with a plate of cake balanced on top, threading his way from the staff room through a new shipment of books to his cataloging corner.

He grinned, his beard rising upward. "Our bread and butter, our raw materials, the reason for our existence."

The term "raw materials" caught Helma's attention. "Raw materials," she repeated, and waited for further explanation. Helma Zukas did not play guessing games.

George was obviously loving every second of the as-yet unexplained turmoil. "Authors," he said with an enthusiastic burst that might have made anyone else take a step backward. "They're objecting to our bestseller table."

She recalled Dutch's dark warning near the bestseller table: "You'll find out," after she'd heard him mumble, "This is what they're mad about."

"Why?" she asked George.

"They claim too many copies of bestsellers are being loaned for free; people won't *buy* their books."

She pictured the titles lining the table, then the faces she'd seen carrying placards. "The authors demonstrating are local authors."

"You got it."

"But none of their books are on the bestseller table."

George guffawed. "It's the principle, Miss Zukas. Think domino, the venerable house of cards: If people don't buy books, bookstores go down; no place to sell your books, so publishers publish fewer books. For want of a nail, and the world of books slams closed in a whimper."

"Certainly they're not demanding the library buy *fewer* books?" Helma asked.

George shrugged. "Don't bring logic into this. Somebody created a formula based on how many books people won't *buy* in relation to the number of copies the library loans for free." He yawned. "They claim we're no longer a service; we're competition."

When Helma entered her cubicle, her mind still toying with the bestseller issue, she heard a flurry of rustling from Harley Woodworth's cubicle next to hers. An object clattered, and Harley popped up over the shelves between their cubicles. He smiled. Helma stared.

"Harley, did you..." She stopped, unsure what to ask—or how to ask it. Harley *wasn't* smirking. His lips were stretched, his eyes unnaturally wide. She finally settled on, "Are you all right, Harley?"

Harley attempted to perform his customary expression of opening his jaws while keeping his lips closed. There was a sound of ripping. Harley winced and slapped a hand to his left jaw, where a strip of clear tape had popped from his skin and dangled loose.

"I thought..." he began in a pained voice, rubbing his face. "I wanted to see what I'd look like if I had...repair work."

"What is it you wish to repair?" she asked, trying to concentrate on a spot at the tip of his nose rather than on his face.

He pointed to his eyes. The left side of Harley's face was normal, the right side stretched straight back. "Just tighten a little here and there."

"How old are you, Harley?"

He looked miserable. "Thirty-three."

"But, Harley——" she began.

"Could you do me a favor?" he asked.

"Certainly, if I can."

He glanced at the wall clock. "I'm scheduled on the reference desk. Can you take my place for five minutes while I..." He pointed to the tape still stretching the right side of his face.

"Of course."

Strains of Handel issued from Ms. Moon's office as Helma passed, and she spotted the director slumped at her desk, her head lying cheek-down on top of open blueprints. Her lips puffed and fluttered in a delicate snore.

"Where's Harley?" Glory Shandy asked when Helma appeared at the reference desk. "It's Harley's turn."

"He's detained for a few minutes."

Glory's lower lip protruded. "It's his turn. I'll wait——"

Across the room, a young woman rose and headed toward the reference desk. Glory jumped up from her chair as the woman opened her mouth, and interjected, "Ask her," pointing to Helma. And she flounced off.

"What's the name of that dancer?" the young woman asked without preamble.

"I beg your pardon."

"You know, the scarf and the Bugatti..." and she raised her hand as if she were hanging herself, sticking out her tongue.

"Isadora Duncan?"

"Right. Thanks."

"I believe we have a biography of her," Helma offered.

"That's okay, I'll look on the internet," she said, heading for the bank of computers.

Lying face-down on the desk blotter was an empty sign holder Ms. Moon had ceremoniously set on the reference desk two weeks earlier. "**Resource Discovery**," it had read. After every librarian had been questioned at least once by patrons wondering where the reference desk had moved to, the sign had mysteriously disappeared. Ms. Moon hadn't noticed.

Helma searched for "Steven Block" and "Seattle" on the computer while she waited for Harley or a library patron, whichever appeared first, but found no credible matches, not with Chip Block nor with permutations of the name Steven, either.

Jaynie Lynn, dressed in a white karate uniform, her braid of glossy hair hanging down her back, was fishing her mail from her mailbox when Helma stopped to retrieve hers.

"You're getting married," Jaynie Lynn said. "Wow. Congratulations."

"Thank you," Helma told her.

"I was married once," Jaynie Lynn continued as she pulled two envelopes and a magazine from her mailbox. She smiled a knowing smile. "Don't believe that 'For-better-and-for-worse-means-for-good' crap. It's a cinch to end it if it doesn't work out." She made a throat-slashing motion.

Helma sorted her mail as she climbed the steps to 3F, ads to the back, bills to the front. The usual: no letters, two solicitations, a grocery store circular. But caught in the pages of the circular was a lumpy envelope with a printed label bearing her name and address. She shook it, feeling a small and hard object sliding inside. There was no return address, nothing written on the back of the envelope, either.

TNT's apartment door opened. "Helma." Beneath TNT's multi-broken nose his mouth stretched in a wide, helpless smile.

"Hello, TNT. You look happy."

"I just had a call from your mother, and your aunt asked to speak to me."

"Oh?"

He nodded and the Irish thickened. "The dear lady invited me to dinner. How about that? I may be finally winning over the old girl after all."

"I think she's always liked you, TNT," Helma told him. "She just worries about Mother."

"Ah." He nodded again, straightening his shoulders and expanding his chest. "Like I'm a wild Irish bounder who might break the poor girl's heart."

Helma smiled, thinking it was more that Aunt Em couldn't bear watching Lillian acting, as she'd claimed in a fit of pique, like an "over-aged tart," but she said, "Did you accept the invitation?"

"Wouldn't miss it. What kind of flowers shall I take her?" Even as he stood in his doorway, his body bobbed and flexed, as if he were about to sprint off down the steps for a five-mile run.

"Aunt Em? Any flower would please her, but she has a special affinity for daisies."

"That's what it'll be, then: daisies." He snapped his fingers and stepped back into his apartment. "Oh," he said, halting, one hand on the doorknob, "I took a rabbit away from your cat. He was trying to drag it up the stairs."

"He killed a full-grown rabbit?"

"Nope. Alive and kicking. Bringing it home for a little sport on your balcony, I'd guess." Admiration passed across TNT's face before he smoothed it to neutral, but still said like a tribute, "He's a hooligan, that cat."

Inside her apartment, after a sweeping glance to be sure all was well, Helma glanced onto the balcony to see Boy Cat Zukas hunkered on the mat, surrounded by a wispish pile of small gray feathers. He blinked at her and continued preening himself. Live rabbit; dead bird.

She gently fingered the anonymous envelope again. Whatever it contained was small, wrapped inside a soft layer that felt like cloth or tissue. Holding it away from her face, she slit the edges with her letter opener, then tipped the envelope and tapped it gently against her counter, emptying it. Out fell a small tissue-wrapped object, neatly taped into a square. There was nothing else in the envelope, no note, no explanation. Perhaps she should call the police? There *had* been a death and robbery after all.

But no, that was silly. The crime didn't have anything to do with Helma. She used a fingernail to peel off the taped edges of the tissue but that tore the tissue and finally she simply ripped it open.

She recognized the contents immediately. Onto her counter rolled a worn and thin gold band, the ring her father had bought her mother during their poverty-filled early days. Her mother's stolen wedding ring.

CHAPTER 9

A Ring of Truth

"May I tell my mother?" Helma asked Wayne Gallant. With gloved hands, he slipped Helma's mother's ring into one plastic evidence bag, and the envelope and tissue it had arrived in, into another.

"If you want. Or you can wait until we do an analysis. She'll be pleased to have it returned, but..." He hesitated. "...she'll have a lot of questions you won't be able to answer."

"I'll wait," Helma decided as she wiped off the counter with a paper towel. "I would have expected the ring to be mailed to my mother, not me. Someone who knew I was her daughter sent it." She thought a moment, pausing to fold the used paper towel into quarters, matching corners. "But *who* sent it to me? Aunt Em's other robber?"

"Maybe," Wayne sealed the evidence bags and pulled off his gloves. Helma was surprised that disposable gloves came in sizes large enough to fit his hands. "Or we could be dealing with an honest person here."

"Honest?" Helma questioned.

He nodded. "Suppose the ring fell out of the alleged robber's pocket when he hit the pavement, and our honest sender picked it up off the ground."

"And then he or she felt they'd garner too much attention if they belatedly turned it into the police."

"So they took it to the post office." He frowned. "They must have mailed it immediately after the crime in order for you to get it today."

"May I see the envelope?"

He laid it on her counter and smoothed the plastic bag with his thumbs.

The envelope was properly addressed to her, and the postage stamp in the upper right corner was a popular "Forever" stamp that would never rise in price. She had purchased five hundred stamps herself just prior to the last postage stamp increase.

"The stamp isn't canceled," she pointed out. "It wasn't mailed; it was slipped into my mailbox. Whoever did it not only knows who I am but also exactly *where* I live."

The chief's hands went still.

"If this came from Aunt Em's other robber, why leave it in *my* mailbox?" she asked. "How would he know my identity?"

"Maybe because you observed him on the scene and didn't realize what you were seeing?" Wayne suggested.

"He *knows* me," Helma whispered. "And believes I may have recognized him, that I could identify him?" She shook her head. "I didn't arrive at the Silver Gables until well after the crime was committed, and the robber who exited through the window was dead. Surely the accomplice would have fled by then. Besides, returning the ring only directs more attention toward him – or her. It wasn't the most logical act."

"No one ever claimed criminals were logical. I think your cat wants in."

Boy Cat Zukas gazed inside, his paws kneading amongst the gray feathers, his mouth stretching wide as if he were meowing. As she opened the sliding door for him and he lazily strode to his wicker basket, she realized that she and Wayne had never discussed cats. She disliked cats herself, but she had taken responsibility for Boy Cat Zukas, and Helma Zukas did not abandon her responsibilities. So naturally, the former alley cat would have to live wherever she did, and with whomever she did. She wouldn't dream of inflicting him on anyone else.

"If the second robber returned my mother's ring in some misguided idea of restitution for his crime, wouldn't he have sent me Aunt Em's *Stelmužė* box, too?"

She paused to step onto her balcony and lift the mat, folding the ends together to contain the scattered feathers. No head or body parts remained, not even a wing. She checked to be sure there was no breeze to blow the feathers onto another balcony below hers, then shook the mat over the railing. The wisps of feathers drifted gently away.

"If he *is* motivated by guilt, murder ranks higher on the guilt scale than theft," Wayne said when she returned, "which reinforces the idea that an uninvolved person may have sent this to you."

"But a person who knows me, who believes I may have witnessed him or her on the scene."

"Maybe. Maybe not. Just keep replaying the scene in your mind," Wayne advised her. "Gently. Don't poke at it. If you saw anything unusual, it'll come back to you."

Many important revelations had come to Helma in just that way – often while she was sleeping or bathing. For instance, the time she'd dozed during her Thursday evening bath and awakened to cold water and a perfect configuration for the library's new DVD collection of PBS nature shows.

"The paper intimated the mayor is putting pressure on your department," Helma told Wayne as she washed her hands at the kitchen sink.

"He'd like to see it solved, and so would we."

"Not to mention there's an election this fall."

Wayne nodded and slipped the sealed evidence bags into his pocket, saying without looking at her, "Do you like large... weddings?"

"I don't mind attending large weddings," Helma told him, "but if it were my own—"

One side of his mouth rose and he rested his hand on her shoulder. "It is."

Helma swallowed, feeling the warm weight of his hand. "What is?"

"The wedding. It *is* your wedding. Our wedding."

"Our wedding," she repeated, forgetting exactly what it was about weddings he'd asked her.

Helma's mother phoned while she was washing their wine-glasses: red residue in his, white in hers. "Em's beside herself, Helma. Can't you speed up the police investigation? I don't know what I'm going to do with her if she doesn't get that silly box back."

"I'm sure they're doing everything they can, Mother. Call Detective Carter if you have any questions. He's the lead investigator."

"But you have a direct line to the chief, dear. You're his future wife. Certainly you have more influence than—"

"TNT said Aunt Em invited him for dinner," Helma interrupted, hoping to send her on another track.

"That's right. She plans to make all that Lithuanian food for him. Potatoes and fat. He'll probably drop dead of a heart attack right at the table. Now, dear..."

"Mother, I..."

"No, no. This is something else." She took a deep breath and Helma braced herself, suspecting she was about to discover the real reason for her mother's telephone call. Lillian's voice turned breezy and light.

"Mister Dubois is willing to see you tomorrow morning. It's the only time he has available. We're so lucky to get an appointment so quickly. You're going to love him."

"Who is Mr. Dubois?" Helma asked, and something in her voice made Boy Cat Zukas lift his head and flash her one of his sharp stares, "And why do I want to see him?"

"I'm sure I've told you about him, dear. He lives up on six, almost a penthouse. He used to do makeovers for the stars."

"And?"

"He also gives beauty advice to new brides. Em was so excited to make an appointment for you. He only sees a select clientele. Very exclusive. You'll love him."

"You said that. But I have no reason to see Mr. Dubois."

Lillian's voice rose. "But you have to. You see, I suggested Mr. Dubois to distract Em from her loss. I had to do *something*. She's the one who talked to him and she's counting on you consulting with him."

"But Mother, I . . ."

"Nine in the morning. Sixth floor."

"Tomorrow's Tuesday. I have to work."

"You're working?"

"Of course."

"Oh dear. Em will be broken-hearted. And just when I thought I had her calmed down from her terrible experience. A dead man – can you imagine how it traumatized her? She was so thrilled about Mr. Dubois, absolutely thrilled. I don't know how I'll tell her you've declined her gift. And then she'll be back in panic city over that silly old box. It can't be good for her heart."

Helma Zukas rarely allowed herself to be manipulated. She sighed, conceding this was going to be one of those times. For Aunt Em she'd see "Mr. Dubois," whoever he was. A quick appointment and that was it. Nothing else.

"All right, Mother, I'll keep the appointment. Thank Aunt Em for me and tell her I'll meet her Mr. Dubois."

"Oh goody. You'll love him," she repeated again, and gaily added before she hung up, "Nine o'clock, sixth floor. Ta-ta."

But no revelations crept into Helma's mind during that night. She slept soundly, peacefully even, undisturbed by dreams or conjecture involving recognizable faces in the crowd around the dead robber, why her mother's stolen ring had been sent to her, who had dared rob Aunt Em, or the perplexing question of how to escape her appointment with Mr. Dubois.

Boy Cat Zukas sat in his wicker basket, turned so his rear faced the room, stone still, the tip of his tail twitching. In his line of vision, two house finches sat on the railing of her balcony, ruffling and fluffing. He made a kak-kak-kak noise as if his teeth were chattering.

Helma drank a full glass of water, part of her morning routine, then poached herself an egg and slid it onto a piece of dry toast, letting Boy Cat Zukas entertain himself before she let him out. The birds flapped into the low-slung sky the instant she approached her sliding glass doors. The cat slunk outside, his eyes focused on the spot where the finches had lately perched.

There was no mention of the dead robber or the robbery in the *Bellehaven Daily News*. The incident had been pushed off the radar: the mayor had bought a new bicycle; schoolteachers were threatening to strike because the salaries of city bus drivers were higher than their own; and a group was petitioning the City to remove the metal cones that kept seagulls from perching on docks, citing "bird stress." No mention of the picketing authors, either.

At 8:05, her breakfast dishes washed and trash emptied, Helma phoned the library to explain she'd be late. When Helma heard Glory Shandy's effusive voice instead of Dutch's measured, if slightly suspicious tones, she could almost see her red curls bouncing.

"How may I help you?" Glory breathed into the phone.

"This is Helma Zukas. I'll be in at ten this morning."

The effusiveness disappeared. "Are you sick?"

"I have an appointment."

"A doctor's appointment?"

"I'll be in at ten," Helma repeated.

"If you're sick, you shouldn't come in at all."

"Thank you. I'll be in at ten," Helma said, and hung up.

Helma shouldn't have been surprised that at 8:55, when she entered the lobby of the Silver Gables on her way to Mr. Dubois's sixth floor "penthouse," she discovered Aunt Em and her mother seated together on a leather sofa that directly faced the front entrance.

Lillian clapped her hands when she spotted Helma and waved her over, her smile wide. "Hello, dear. We're just enjoying the morning. Beautiful day, isn't it?"

Since the day was currently gray, notwithstanding the weatherman's doubtful promise of "sunbreaks," and since Lillian rarely rose before nine, Helma approached them with hesitation.

Aunt Em, on the other hand, had lost the need to sleep any regular hours and was as likely to be found baking cookies at two a.m. as having retired for the night at four o'clock in the afternoon.

"Does your policeman know my *Stelmužė* box is missing?" Aunt Em asked. She held a white business-size envelope in her hand, and her lipstick was bleeding into the creases rising from her upper lip.

Lillian rolled her eyes and answered before Helma. "Of course he does. He's her fiancé."

"That does not mean he knows," Aunt Em said stubbornly.

"He knows, Aunt Em," Helma told her. "He's working very hard to find it for you."

"You're here for your appointment with Mr. Dubois," Lillian said. 'Ooh, I can't wait to hear his - "

Lillian stopped and glanced over Helma's shoulder. "Run along, dear," she prompted with uncharacteristic urgency. "Don't be late. Come back and tell us all about it."

"Back to our apartment," Aunt Em added, also with a "run-along-now" tone. Helma kissed them both and didn't look behind her until she reached the door to the stairs. Then she turned and peered toward the front door, searching for whatever had captured Lillian and Aunt Em's attention.

A man, who she at first thought was one of the young gardeners who kept up the Silver Gables' grounds, stood just inside the double doors. He was dressed in jeans and a blue sweatshirt. His hair was pale and longish, and he wore a wispy beard of young blond hair that was nearly invisible. He glanced around the lobby, appearing unsure and out of place. Aunt Em raised her hand in a summoning gesture, attracting his attention, and the young man's shoulders relaxed. He strode across the lobby to them.

And then Aunt Em gave the man the white envelope she'd been holding. He stuffed it in his jeans pocket without opening it and handed her a pink shoebox, then bobbed his head and pivoted to hurriedly exit the front door. Not five words had passed between them. No friendly acknowledgement or smiles, either.

Lillian took Aunt Em's arm and helped her rise. She cradled the pink box to her bosom. The two women slowly made their way toward the elevator, and Helma stepped through the fire door into the stairwell, out of their sight. What had she just witnessed?

Aunt Em's envelope had been flat, as if it held a single piece of paper. A check? Cash? The man had held out his hand for the envelope before he gave her the pink box. Whatever the transaction had been, neither Aunt Em nor Helma's mother had wanted Helma to see it.

Pink, she thought, and definitely resembling a shoebox. What came in a pink shoebox that her mother and Aunt Em would want to hide from her? Certainly they hadn't bought her a gift of wedding shoes, had they? None of the UPS or FedEx, or even postal delivery people she'd dealt with ever expected to be handed an envelope before a delivery. It didn't make sense.

And then she was at the top of the Silver Gables: floor six. She would *definitely* stop by her mother's apartment after she told Mr. Dubois thank you but no thank you.

The door was flung open before Helma could press the doorbell button beside it.

"You're Emily's niece. Ah, the resemblance. *Magnifico!*" The tone was confident, the accent unidentifiable.

In front of Helma stood a man shorter than she was. Unless it was a clever toupee, his bright blond hair was combed back into elegant sleekness. His forehead was blandly smooth, his cheeks deeply furrowed. He wore a white silk shirt, pale linen pants and shiny ecru loafers. The aura of Somewhere Else hovered about him.

Before Helma could affirm her identity, he said, "Let me observe," raising a hand to cup his chin and regarding her from her feet to the stubborn curl on the left side of her head. "I don't know," he said, almost a moan. "I don't know. Come in and we'll assess what can be done." He gave her a slow, pitying smile.

"Mr. Dubois," Helma began, "I appreciate your making an appointment for my mother and aunt, but——"

"They were desperate," he said, and his voice held such a note of sadness Helma felt an unreasonable desire to apologize. "I can see why. I'm not sure how much I can do. But for your aunt… Inside, inside."

And without intending to, she found herself inside his apartment. Her first impression was white.

He circled her. "Good hair," he said. "You've kept yourself in shape for your age."

"I'm not planning—"

"No need to explain. Too many women…" With his hands he made swelling motions over his abdomen, patted the air around his hips. Again, that sad smile.

"Lovely skin. What lotion do you use for your…complexion?" He asked it delicately, as if it might be a secret she'd be reluctant to divulge.

Helma named a time-tested and low-cost hand and body lotion.

Mr. Dubois pursed his lips. "On your *face*? Do you know the difference between those drug store lotions and the finer, signature products?"

"I believe it's mainly cost," she said, recalling research she'd ordered for a chemical engineering grad student who'd been overwhelmed by the university library and fled to the Bellehaven Public Library, instead.

He responded with a brief grunt and click of his tongue.

His apartment was stark. A single white sofa and matching chair, a pale wooden table with two chairs, a small television sitting on a coffee table. He saw her glancing over his furnishings and said airily, "I prefer a minimalist lifestyle. I live like a late Picasso drawing but my designs are of his early years."

"Blue?" Helma couldn't stop herself from asking.

"A humorist," he said.

"Librarian," she told him.

"That explains it," he said. "I'm very busy."

"That's good because I don't believe—"

"Very. I'm not sure I can fit you in."

She spotted only one photograph, and it hung over the sofa in a gold, poster-size frame. A glossy young Mr. Dubois stood behind a woman sitting in a stylist's chair. She looked vaguely familiar. It was signed with a drawn red heart as thick as a lipstick smear, and the single name, "Veronica."

"That's only one example of my work," he said. "And you know what she went on to do." His tone left no room for an admittance of ignorance.

"Then we agree," Helma said. "You're far too busy and my wedding plans are at least a year away."

"Ah, but for Emily I've agreed to orchestrate your transformation. For the beautiful Emily." He gave his head a small shake as if in wonder.

"I'm only here because of Aunt Em's request," Helma told him.

"I see you in cream satin," he said, gazing upward as if his vision hovered at ceiling height, "a simple princess waistline. If we upsweep your hair, clean out your eyebrows, highlight your bone structure. A touch of ochre mascara." He nodded to himself. "Mm-hmm. Classical all the way."

"Do you have...testimonials from other clients?" Helma asked.

He waved his hand vaguely toward the south. "None in this town, naturally. My work takes me back to places where women are more ... conscious of their appearance."

"How much is my aunt paying you for this appointment?"

He held his finger to his lips as if she'd cursed in a child's presence. "It is a gift from them to you, her beloved daughter, her cherished niece. A gift."

"Are you aware of their robbery?"

"And the sad ending of the young man." He nodded. "A tragedy. Your aunt blames herself, but she is very wrong."

"Had you ever seen the deceased man before?" Helma asked. Something in his expression led her to believe he'd viewed the body. "Perhaps visiting someone in the building?"

"No. No. Your mother has a charmingly naughty expression..." He raised his eyebrows at her.

"NOKD," Helma provided. It was an expression her mother had heard on a British comedy and for a brief time had taken to using. *Not our kind, dear*, it meant.

He folded his hands together and eyed Helma expectantly. She should walk out; she should tell him she wasn't returning; she should ask him to give Aunt Em her money back.

But Helma was a keen observer, and while she would never claim to understand Mr. Dubois, she was beginning to have an inkling. "My mother didn't realize I was working today. May I have your card and we'll make another appointment for a day when I have more time?"

He produced a business card from his pocket and presented it to her to pluck from the palm of his hand. It was handmade: "Mr. Dubois" written in elaborate script, with only the word "Beauty" beneath it, followed by his telephone number. "Shall we say Thursday after you've finished your work day at the library? Now that I've seen you, I'll have appropriate samples for your consideration."

"And these samples will consist of...?" Helma asked.

"Ah, wait and see. I believe we will work well together," and he actually bent low as if to kiss her hand. When she took a step backward he modified his stance to a courteous bow from the waist.

CHAPTER 10

Food for Thought

Helma's mother opened the door of her apartment. "Oh, Helma. Didn't you just love Mr. Dubois? He's so refined, so sought after. And he made room for *you*." Behind her wafted the perfume of baking *kugelis*. Helma took a deep breath and felt her stomach rumble.

"Does anyone else in the Silver Gables consult with Mr. Dubois?" She stepped into the apartment, surreptitiously looking for the pink box she'd seen pass between the man and Aunt Em in the lobby. It wasn't anywhere in sight.

"He has so little time. No one here has been able to make an appointment yet. And he flies off a lot." She leaned forward and said in a near whisper. "He's still in demand in the movie business, you know. Very exclusive." She laughed. "Oh, you should hear the wicked stories he can tell."

"How long have you known him?"

"A while." Lillian dismissed time with a wave of her hand. "Long enough."

"About the robbery, Mother."

Lillian gave an extravagant, nearly comic shudder. "That's behind us now, all fuss and feathers."

Helma stared. Yes, her mother had used a phrase of TNT's, even imbuing it with an Irish lilt.

"Did you hear of any other robberies in the building?"

"Dorie Porter said her VISA card was stolen, but she forgot I was with her when she lost it in Wal-Mart last month."

Aunt Em stepped from the rear of the apartment, blinking as if she'd been napping, her hair ragged on the left side of her head. She wore a Mother Hubbard apron.

"You're cooking, Aunt Em," Helma said.

Her aunt nodded and, as if the nod had upset her balance, steadied herself with a hand against the wall. "The boxer is coming for dinner tonight. I'm teaching Lillian how to feed him."

"I can make *kugelis*," Lillian said. Helma knew her mother's *kugelis*; it was gummy, not as crispy on the edges or as light as Aunt Em's. Her father had always eaten a piece or two and then requested Aunt Em, his sister, to make a new batch for him. "Besides, TNT's Irish. It's in his genes to love potatoes in any form."

"It's better when it's cooked right," Aunt Em told her as she shuffled to the stove, one hand trailing against the wall.

"Then you should have told me years ago about the milk."

Helma saw the guilty flicker in Aunt Em's eyes as she said, "I forgot."

Lillian sniffed.

"Where's Ruthie?" Aunt Em asked Helma.

"Probably still in bed this time of morning."

"She is unhappy," her aunt said, a statement, not a question, and opened the oven to peer inside.

"Why do you say that?" Helma asked.

Aunt Em closed the oven door and patted the stove as if it were a good pet. "Ah, a woman with experience understands Ruth's face."

"Who was the man in the lobby?"

"What man?" Lillian questioned too hurriedly.

"He gave a pink box to Aunt Em after she handed him an envelope."

"Ask her," Lillian said, nodding toward Aunt Em.

Aunt Em innocently blinked. "When were we in the lobby? I don't remember any man."

"He gave you a pink box," Helma tried, "the size of a shoebox."

"I bought shoes in the lobby?"

"No. A young man gave you a pink box just as I was leaving the lobby to meet with Mr. Dubois. The box was the size of a shoebox."

Aunt Em shook her head. "I don't know of this box, Wilhelmina. But has your policeman found my *Stelmužė* box?"

Helma surrendered for the moment. "Not yet. But he will. Did you recall anything I can tell the chief about the second robber?"

"There were *two* robbers?" Aunt Em asked, raising her hands to her mouth.

The old and the new and the forgotten had melded in Aunt Em's mind, and Helma let that subject drop, too.

"Mr. Dubois called you 'the beautiful Emily,'" she told Aunt Em.

"Hah," was her only comment.

"Look, Helma." Lillian pointed to her computer screen. "I've begun a guest list for you."

Helma peered over her mother's shoulder, trying to evince interest when all she felt was dread. There on the screen was a list of names under the heading, "Wayne and Helma." The first two guests were Lillian and TNT, followed by Aunt Em.

"Mother, the wedding's at least a year away."

"That doesn't mean the guest list will change." She huffily blinked off the computer screen with a stab of her finger. "I'm only trying to use my skills to be helpful."

There was that sensation again: the urge to curl up for a brief nap. "And I appreciate it. It *will* be helpful to have a guest list already in production," she told her mother, who looked slightly mollified.

"Close up your machinery so we can set the table," Aunt Em told Lillian.

Lillian glanced at the kitchen clock. "Em, TNT won't be here for eight hours."

"A girl should *look* prepared," Aunt Em said, "whether she is or not. Surprises aren't always good."

Lillian walked Helma to the door, talking the while about finger sandwiches and bisques. Helma motioned her into the hallway.

"Then you agree the crab bisque is too messy?" Lillian asked, making soup-scooping motions. "Should we ask Wayne what he thinks?"

"Mother," Helma waited until her mother's eyes finally focused on her own. "I saw the exchange between Aunt Em and the man in the lobby, with the pink box. What was it?"

Lillian's mouth tightened. She rolled her eyes. "You have to ask her."

"I did. She's confused."

"Not as much as she pretends." Lillian nodded to a woman in matching pink sweatpants and hooded sweatshirt, wearing bracelet weights. "Have a good one, Callie."

"Aunt Em didn't buy something for me, did she? The man wasn't delivering a gift?"

Lillian snorted. "Hardly. It's all her own doing and I'm tired of it."

"Tell me."

Lillian stubbornly shook her head. "An old lady like her. I'm embarrassed and I'm not going to keep covering for her. Not when my daughter's marrying the chief of police."

"Aunt Em is involved in an activity that's *illegal*?" Helma asked, suddenly remembering Dalia's ridiculous-seeming question about gangs.

"Shh," Lillian cautioned, nodding her head toward the door across the hall, which looked tightly closed to Helma. "You talk to her later. Make her tell you. I have to go back in and make sure she doesn't dish out food on the plates six hours too early." And Lillian kissed Helma's cheek and re-entered her apartment.

Immediately, the door of Mrs. Caldecott's apartment next door opened and Mrs. Caldecott leaned out. She no longer wore the pink curlers, but her silver hair retained their rounded shape as if she hadn't combed out her curls.

"How's Em?" she asked, sotto voce.

"How are you, Mrs. Caldecott?" Helma asked.

The woman nodded. "Better. Do you like our Mr. Dubois?"

"I hardly know him," Helma said noncommittally, marveling anew at the speed of even non-news.

"Well, everybody says he's magic. Not that I'm the sort of woman he'd want to work his magic on." And she laughed in a self-deprecating way.

"Do you know any of his clients?"

"Heavens, no." Mrs. Caldecott untwirled one of the sausage curls. "Movie stars and all those kinds of people."

"It's good to see the building has returned to normal after Sunday's events," Helma said.

"Oh, yes. The excitement's over now. The police were here this morning asking if I was robbed, too."

"Did you hear if anyone else in the Silver Gables was a victim?" Helma asked, watching her closely.

"Not on this floor."

At the other end of the hall, the elevator dinged and Helma heard a trio of children's voices singing, "Going to see our grandma, our grandma, our grandma, 'cause she's not dead like our grandpa, our grandpa, our grandpa."

"She was looking for you. I told her you had a doctor's appointment, and if you came in at all, it wouldn't be before ten," Glory Shandy said as Helma walked past Glory's cubicle on the way to her own.

Helma only nodded and continued walking. There was no point in clarifying facts with Glory. But Glory followed behind her in a rustle and flourish. She wore yellow tights and a dress with butterflies flitting across it. A clip that looked curiously like a monarch butterfly pupa held back her red curls. Her makeup, with a round circle of pink on each cheek, projected a Raggedy Ann affect. "Do the police know any more about the man your aunt murdered?"

Helma stopped. "I beg your pardon?"

"Oh." Glory clasped one of her small hands over her mouth and batted her eyes. "Did I say something wrong? I didn't mean to upset you. Maybe I misunderstood."

"Yes, I believe you did." Helma set her bag and purse on her desk, and with her attention interrupted by Glory, her usually acute sense of spatial relationships faltered. Her purse slid off the edge of her desk and clattered to the floor, contents spilling. She bent to retrieve her possessions at the same time as Glory and they bumped shoulders. "I can get it, thank you," Helma told her.

"You're seeing him?" Glory squealed, and Helma saw she held Mr. Dubois's card. "Is he your wedding planner?"

"Do you know Mr. Dubois?" Helma reached for the card, but Glory pulled it closer to her heart.

"I've heard he can work miracles. My hair stylist told me about him. He's new to Bellehaven, but he came from California and he worked with..." Glory's voice hushed to reverence. "... movie stars." She narrowed her eyes at Helma. "How long have you been going to him?"

"I'm not 'going to him,' Glory. Now if you'll excuse me, did you say Ms. Moon wanted to see me?"

Glory frowned. "Ms. Moon?" She shook her head and something jingled in her hair. "Oh. Not Ms. Moon. Your friend, Ruth Winthrop."

Glory was drawn to Ruth in curious awe. Ruth's size or flash, or perhaps her obvious disdain for Glory, lured the younger librarian like a magnet. When Ruth wore her normal high heels, Glory barely reached Ruth's elbow.

"Where is Ruth?"

"Out there. With Dutch." She pointed toward the door to the public area.

"Thank you," Helma said, gently removing Mr. Dubois's card from Glory's hand. Her eyes followed it to Helma's purse.

The library wouldn't open to the public for another ten minutes. Helma found Ruth leaning on the circulation counter talking to Dutch, who was labeling carts of returned books for the pages to reshelve. Ruth wore a yellow cowboy hat.

"Hey, Helma. Dutch knows the dead guy."

"Steven Block?"

"Tell her, Dutch."

Dutch stood ramrod straight as if reporting on a military maneuver. "I remember him because of the name: Chip Block. I volunteer at the mission and he signed in last week for dinner."

"Alone?" Helma asked.

"Appeared to be."

"Did he spend the night?"

"Couldn't say. Ask Brother Danny."

"Have you told the police?"

Dutch shook his head. "I don't call them; they don't call me."

Bethany, the library's most recently hired page, entered the circulation area and pulled one of the book trucks out of line.

Dutch glanced at the clock and said, "Bethany, your shift doesn't start for forty minutes."

Bethany continued pushing the book truck toward the stacks, saying over her shoulder, "I thought I'd start early so I wouldn't have so much to do."

Ruth waved toward the workroom door and Helma spotted Glory backing through the door as if she'd been caught spying. "Munchkin," Ruth muttered.

"You wanted to see me, Ruth?"

"Not really. Seeya, Dutch."

Dutch waved his hand briskly from his fleet of book trucks where he stood shaking his head after Bethany, and Ruth pulled Helma toward the front doors. Three book and laptop–laden people already stood waiting for Dutch to unlock the doors. Ruth gave them a cheery wave, and they scowled through the glass at her. "You won't believe the curious thing that happened a little while ago."

Helma waited.

"Don't you want to hear it?"

"I'm sure you're going to tell me."

Ruth rolled her eyes. "Yeah, yeah. Well, don't overexcite yourself. Who should appear on my doorstep an hour ago but our favorite detective, Carter Houston. I wasn't even awake yet. He's lucky—or should I say unlucky—that I found my robe."

"What did he want?"

"That's exactly what he asked me."

"You called Carter, Ruth?"

"Not a chance. He claimed he'd received a message saying I had valuable information for him about the robbery."

"Who'd given him the message?"

"I couldn't pry it out of him. Police confidentiality and all that—or so he alleged. I think it was a ploy to barge inside my house and look for contraband." A man wearing a backpack tapped on the library's plate glass door and Ruth pointed to her wrist as if she wore a watch, holding up two fingers.

"Did you let Carter inside?"

"Almost. He seemed so sincere." She frowned and pulled a strand of her black wiry hair, a sign of uncertainty for Ruth. "Sincere for Carter, anyway. In the end I told him to be more specific or come back with a search warrant."

"And?"

"He huffed and puffed and drove away in his little black car."

It was unusual behavior for the always correct, always specific Carter Houston. "I believe him," Helma said. "He's too fastidious in his work to appear on your doorstep without a legitimate reason."

Had the person who'd sent Lillian's wedding ring to Helma also passed information about Ruth to Carter? Someone manipulating behind the scenes?

Ruth shrugged. "Maybe it was that witnessing-without-realizing theory mentioned by your husband-to-be. You know, robber number two tripped over my feet as we were viewing his buddy's body and I just didn't recognize him as the potential crook I sat next to at Joker's three weeks ago. Carter always suspects the worst."

"*Do* you recall anything unusual?" Helma asked. She herself had repeatedly gone over the crime scene, attempting to envision the faces in the crowd, from their arrival at the Silver Gables until they'd fled her mother's apartment following Ruth's announcement of Helma's engagement.

"Other than seeing a dead man four stories below me with a television set perched on his body? Nope."

Someone was playing with them. Was it the criminal, taunting them because he was confident he wouldn't be caught? Aunt Em and Lillian might have been just one segment of a mysterious felony, or perhaps *several* planned felonies, and somehow Helma and Ruth were involved.

She briefly considered and rejected the idea that the anonymous person who'd delivered her mother's ring and sent the police to Ruth's was providing hints about the crime without throwing any suspicion on himself, that the person or persons was actually trying to *help*. It was just too coy.

"What's that about?" Ruth asked, breaking into Helma's reverie.

Helma looked up. The authors were back. Five or six of them milling on the library's front steps, carrying backpacks and thermoses and placards. They peered into the library. One of them, a tall woman with gray hair, jabbed a forefinger toward the table of multiple bestsellers behind Helma, her mouth working.

"Authors," Helma told Ruth. "They're upset about the library's bestseller table." Helma didn't point inside buildings but simply told Ruth, "Behind you."

Ruth walked around the table laden with bright multiple copies of bestsellers. "Wow. What's this for?"

"We're assuring the public we can satisfy their reading desires without overly long waits," Helma said, wincing as she recognized Ms. Moon's words dropping from her lips, which in their staff meeting had been followed by George nudging Harley and whispering, "Instant gratification has always worked for me."

Ruth made quotation marks in the air and intoned as if she were reading a headline, "Bookstore Goes Bankrupt. 'Why buy a bestseller?' former customer asks. 'I don't have to wait—or pay—at my library.' "

Although Ruth was exaggerating, she touched on Helma's niggling, uncomfortable feeling about the new bestseller program: that siphoning money into bestsellers wasn't the library's role, that there *was* a hazy domino effect that reached back to bookstores, publishers, and authors. But then, what *was* the library's role in these days of instantly accessible information?

"I wonder if they need an extra body?" Ruth mused, gazing out at the gathering authors with a gleam in her eyes.

"You're not an author," Helma reminded her.

"Creative is creative. Words, paint—it's all the same bucket. I could lead them in a rousing song of solidarity."

Helma pictured Ruth outside the library, marching, waving a placard and intimidating library patrons. "I have something to tell you," she said.

"Horrors. Are you playing guessing games with me?"

"Not at all. It's something I received in my mail box yesterday."

"Your mother's wedding ring?" Ruth said after Helma described the anonymous envelope. "That's bizarre. And no note. Let's see the ring."

"I gave it to the police."

"Which policeman? Not Carter? Was that why he showed up on my doorstep: he thought I sent it?"

"I gave it to Wayne. It's being tested for fingerprints."

"It's the thief, pleading to be caught. Or maybe he has a misplaced guilty conscience. It's okay to snuff out his partner, but he feels real sorry he robbed two old ladies?"

Dutch unlocked the library's front doors and a stream of patrons entered the building. The book-return door thumped, the computers came alive, and Helma heard Glory's bright voice asking from the reference desk, "How may I help *you*?"

"Are you familiar with a Mr. Dubois?" Helma asked Ruth.

"The makeup guy?" The authors stayed outside, filing slowly up and down the sidewalk, stopping every now and then to greet people and extend what looked like a petition on a clipboard. "Heard of him but never had the pleasure. I do my own."

Overdo, some people claimed.

"Why?" She gazed suspiciously at Helma. "You're not planning to go to him, are you?"

"My mother and Aunt Em made an appointment with him for me."

Ruth guffawed. "You can't be ser – " Ruth snapped her mouth closed, and Helma grew aware of Glory edging up on them from the direction of the reference desk, her eyes as bright on Ruth as a game hunter's. When Glory was within hearing, Ruth raised her arms and said to Helma in a loud, and, well, *awed* voice oozing with insincerity, *"Mr. Dubois?* How did you manage that? I've tried for *years* to get an appointment with him. He's absolutely miraculous."

Helma didn't think Mr. Dubois had resided in Bellehaven for years. Only a few months in the Silver Gables.

"Oh," Glory cried, standing close to Ruth and gazing up at her as if all knowledge resided there. "I heard you. You were talking about Mr. Dubois…"

"Very exclusive," Ruth whispered, and Glory eagerly nodded. "He's dedicating all his resources to Helma right now. Maybe when Helma's satisfied with his …ministrations, he can book you in."

This had gone far enough. "Ruth," Helma began, but she was interrupted by Ms. Moon, who joined them, her hands clasped, asking in a tremulous voice, "Shall I call the police?"

The director, whose weight had once again melted away— "Stomach removal: snip, snip," George had speculated—had recently taken to wearing wide belts that cut her body into segments like a yellowjacket wasp. She also now favored low-cut tops that bared an expanse of freckled bosom.

Glory gasped; Ruth said, "Huh?" and Helma asked, "Has a crime occurred that we need the police?"

"What if they turn violent?" Ms. Moon asked, nodding toward the picketing authors. One of them had opened a TV tray on the sidewalk and was offering copies of his book for sale. **20% Off Today Only**, the sign taped to his TV tray read.

"Authors wouldn't turn violent," Glory said fervently, clasping her hands over her heart in imitation of Ms. Moon.

"I don't know," Ruth said. "Have you read some of that stuff they write?"

"To call the police on authors in front of the public library might not be the image we wish to project," Helma told Ms. Moon.

"You're right," Ms. Moon said, nodding. "I'll have to think of something else."

"You could go out and talk to them, explain the library's policy," Helma suggested.

Ms. Moon shook her head and gestured vaguely from the authors to herself, "I'm not dressed for it." She wandered off toward the workroom, Glory trailing behind her.

Ruth watched them depart, a slight smile on her face. "I love this place."

"Many people love their library. It's even an ALA slogan: 'Heart your library.' There are bumper stickers."

"You misunderstand," Ruth said. "I love *this* place."

CHAPTER 11

Czar or Tsar?

"Let's drop in at the police station and inform our favorite lawmen that Chip off the Block stayed at the mission. Maybe he left clues scattered around the building. Not only that, we can find out whose fingerprints are on your mother's ring."

"I'm scheduled for the reference desk in a few minutes," Helma told Ruth, glancing at her watch, "but I can take a short break after that."

"I'm not sure I can wait." Ruth twisted her hands together, and Helma heard the impatient tapping of her feet. "I'm jumpy, you know what I mean?"

Helma did not believe in being "jumpy," but she was familiar with Ruth's version of jumpiness, and it was never good. "Can you read a few art books until I'm finished?"

"Looking at art right now hurts my stomach. I used to make art. People once bought my art, remember? Paid good money for it. Now I can't even make schlock." She drooped. "It's over. Whatever I used to be, it's over."

"Only temporarily, Ruth. You've felt this way in the past. It always comes back."

"Don't patronize me. I'll go sit over there and wait for you." Ruth pointed toward the dwindling magazine collection. "I might read about cooking."

As far as Helma knew, Ruth's cooking experience outside of heating prepared food in her microwave, consisted of toasting marshmallows over her gas burner. "Good idea," she said.

On the reference desk, Helma answered questions about ebooks, fixed the printer three times, asked a man to eat his smoked salmon and crackers outside, and quelled a quarrel between a man and woman over which of them had sat down at a computer first. "Couldn't you have left something to say you were using this computer?" the woman demanded of the man who claimed he'd just stepped away to use the restroom. "It's not like I carry a purse," he retorted, and it escalated from there.

"I need that new book on relationship advice," a woman holding a spiral notebook requested, "the one with the heart on the cover."

While Helma found an array of appropriate titles in the online catalog, she kept half an ear on the woman's story about someone named 'Ted.' "We finish each other's sentences," she informed Helma.

Yes, Helma thought to herself. That would be irritating.

Real questions were becoming a rarity. No longer: what's the largest city in Turkey, who signed the Declaration of Independence, how do you remove blood stains, what's the gestation period of a leopard, how do hummingbirds migrate. Whether the answers were correct or not, most people checked the internet first.

Helma skimmed through the usual articles of *Library Journal*—which the library now subscribed to online to avoid, as Ms. Moon had announced, glancing meaningfully at George Melville, "the unfortunate habit of some staff members to monopolize the journal." She tried to banish conjecture of Aunt Em and her mother's robbery, or the dead Chip Block, or—she rubbed her forehead—the growing swirl around her... wedding.

Loud whispering interrupted her thoughts and she glanced toward the magazine section. Ruth was chatting to a man seated beside her. Even sitting, he was obviously tall—Ruth's first criteria in matters of male/female interaction. He sat primly, with his long legs pressed together, as if he were a man accustomed to balancing a laptop.

"Excuse me, miss."

Helma looked up into the face of an elderly man with brilliant blue eyes. He was stoop-shouldered and his hands shook with a slight palsy. "Of course, how may I help you?"

"I'd like to find detailed information on the Russian Revolution."

Helma felt the rising Thrill of the Search. "I can show you several," she said, pushing back her chair. "Is there a specific aspect of the Russian Revolution you're interested in?"

And so it went, as she guided him to the 900's section of the Dewey Decimal collection, narrowing and refining his needs through a well-conducted reference interview, supplying a historical atlas with maps, finding a photographic history of the Romanovs, pointing out possible journal articles, her cheeks increasingly flushed with pleasure and her heart singing in librarian ecstasy.

Finally, they were finished, and after thanking her profusely, he headed for the circulation desk, rosy-cheeked and smiling, carrying a stack of relevant material in his arms.

Warm from a successfully-executed reference encounter, Helma watched him depart. He paused by the magazine section where Ruth still chatted with the tall blond man, and pointedly cleared his throat. The young man looked up, nodded, and rose after a brief exchange with Ruth.

Something about the way he pivoted away from Ruth toward the elderly man caught Helma's attention. She studied him. As he passed the reference desk, she realized that the bright light from the library's windows had obscured the wispy fair hair on his chin. He had a blond beard.

It was the same young man who'd given Aunt Em the pink shoebox.

CHAPTER 12

Fighting for the Arts

Helma knew it was an illusion: every minute lasted sixty seconds. But it felt like hours until George arrived to relieve her at the reference desk. Ruth still sat in the magazine area, her head back in one of the new blue plastic reading chairs that resisted hair oil, dirt, lice, and hopefully bed bugs. A child stood in front of her, watching her snore.

She could have looked in the library's computerized circulation program for the name of the elderly man who'd borrowed the Russian Revolution materials, and then perhaps searched his name and found a connection to the young blond man. A son? Grandson? She could have. The computer screen sat on the desk in front of her, her fingers hovering over the keyboard. But Helma Zukas believed in the privacy of library patrons and the tenets of the American Library Association. She resolutely removed her hands from the keyboard and folded them tightly in her lap until her fingers began to ache. She would not do it.

But she could have.

"Here to relieve you, ma'am," George said in mock military fashion. "All quiet on the reference front?"

"Computer number 24 keeps freezing, but everything else is normal," Helma told him. "I'm taking a break now."

"Gotcha," George said, setting a pile of materials on the desk. He grinned sheepishly and tucked a Manga comic book back into the stack until it was invisible. "Ruth said you had an angle on the dead guy."

"At this point it's unconfirmed information," Helma told him.

"If Dutch said it, consider it confirmed." He nodded toward Ruth, who'd just gargled a hefty snore and sent the child watching her into a fit of giggles. "Gonna have a sore throat."

Ruth didn't wake up until Helma gave up whispering her name or gently nudging her shoulder, and finally pinched her wrist with a serious tweak of her fingers. And then Helma had to step back fast when Ruth sat up and swatted the air.

"What's going on?" she demanded, and even in today's modern library where people no longer whispered or kept their voices low, and sometimes sang along unnoticed to music on headsets, several patrons raised their eyes at Ruth's outburst.

"We're going to the police station, remember?" Helma reminded Ruth in a low voice. "To inform them of Chip Block."

Ruth blinked rapidly. "Oh yeah. His sojourn at the mission. Let's go, then," she said as if she'd been the one impatiently waiting.

Helma had to choose between exiting the library through the workroom where they were liable to run into Glory and Ms. Moon, or through the front door where it was necessary to walk through the gauntlet of picketing authors. She chose the front door. A wan light, almost one of the promised sunbreaks, formed a hazy nimbus in the gray sky.

"Care to sign our petition to bring equal purchasing rights to the library?" the woman holding the clipboard asked. "We..." She stepped back. "Oh, you're one of the librarians."

"Yes, I am," Helma acknowledged.

The woman hugged her clipboard and blocked Helma's path. "How can you justify mass purchases of over-popular, literary-deficient books? Do you realize you're a locally-funded, public institution supporting mainstream authors to the detriment of—"

"Hey," Ruth interrupted, stepping between Helma and the woman. "Can I sign your petition?"

"Certainly," she said, handing the clipboard to Ruth, who Helma could see was writing her name large enough to cover two lines.

"If you win this," Ruth asked, "will you take on library art?"

"How?" The woman looked confused but eager to help.

"Pull down that second-rate Van Gogh print over the magazine racks and put up a local artist's work. You know the one I mean?"

"I'm not sure."

"Well, take a look next time you're inside. You'll see. Good luck."

They passed through the protesting authors without further assault.

"How's the Moonbeam going to placate them?" Ruth asked, glancing over her shoulder at the authors. "She'll have to come up with something better than having them all arrested."

"She's formulating a response now, I'm sure," Helma said hopefully. "Who was that man you were talking to in the magazine section?"

"What'd he look like?"

"Tall, blond. Young. He had an unkempt beard."

"'Unkempt,' Helma? 'Unkempt'? I didn't get his name."

"Does he live in Bellehaven?" They passed three teenagers sitting on a planter, and who hid their hands behind their backs as Ruth and Helma drew even with them.

Ruth shrugged.

"Where does he work?" Helma asked in exasperation.

"He didn't tell me. Why? You're engaged to be married, remember?"

"He looked familiar to me, that's all." She had yet to tell Ruth about the man delivering the pink shoebox to Aunt Em in the Silver Gables lobby.

"So ask him yourself." They turned into the sidewalk that led to the main entrance of the police station. A group of preschoolers, each with a hand on a rope and following a young teacher who held the other end, exited the station, appearing unnaturally subdued. Seeing them, Helma remembered a picture book she'd loved as a child and mentally recited, "Jack, Kack, Lack, Mack, Nack, Oack, Pack, and Quack."

"I don't know who he is, Ruth. That's why I asked you."

"I'm meeting him at Joker's at seven tonight. What do you want me to find out?"

"Nothing. As I said, he looked familiar."

"Sure."

A new receptionist, who wore a button with a smiley-face above the words "In Training," sat at the front desk. "How do you spell your name?" she asked Helma when they told her which case they were referring to, biting her lip as she recorded it.

Helma spelled Zukas for her, and Ruth unnecessarily added, "She's engaged to the chief."

"Oh," the receptionist said, setting down her pen and inspecting Helma with a cool look. "Camella told me about you. Just a second," and she spoke into her phone.

Ruth raised her eyebrows at Helma and unaccountably whispered, "Ouch."

"He'll be right out," she said, and three minutes later, Carter Houston entered the lobby from the rear of the building, tugging down the sleeves of his black suit jacket.

Ruth groaned and gave the detective a tooth-baring smile. "They really did put you in charge of this case, didn't they, Carter?"

"Miss Zukas, Miss Winthrop," he said, ignoring Ruth's comment. "Come on back."

Carter's office was as tidy as he was: even the chair he'd just vacated was pushed squarely into his desk. Manila file folders were neatly closed and aligned, a pen and pencil positioned at the edge of his blotter. Helma sat in an upholstered chair at an angle from his desk, totally comfortable in his space.

"How may I help you?" he asked in the same tone the librarians used to greet library patrons, all of them victims of the same city-wide personnel workshops.

"Here in the sanctity of your realm, Carter," Ruth launched off, hands gesticulating, her chin jutting forward, "you can tell us who sent you to grill me this morning, and what it was about. Did you think I was hiding aliens or something?"

"Police business, Miss Winthrop." Carter spoke with finality, even dismissing Ruth with his eyes, settling instead on Helma.

Ruth exhaled as if she were cooling her forehead. "Okay, so do you want to know where the dead guy spent the night before Helma's aunt killed him?"

It was a futile effort, but Helma said it anyway, "Aunt Em did not kill the robber, Ruth, and we don't know first-hand where he spent the night."

"As good as — in both instances," Ruth said stubbornly, then paused before she announced, "At the mission." She grinned at Carter smugly. "What do you think of that?"

Carter didn't answer for a few seconds. He looked at Ruth with no change in expression, but Helma saw the tiny twitch in his right eye. "Yes, we're aware of his time at the mission."

Helma, as observant of human nature as she was of disorder, thought, *Why is he lying?*

Ruth visibly deflated. "You do? Who told you? What was he doing there?"

"That is privileged police information," Carter repeated stiffly, "but thank you for bringing it to our attention."

"Yeah, good citizen that I am," Ruth said. "Let's go, Helm. This was a bust." She stood up.

"Did you find any fingerprints on my mother's ring, or any evidence on the envelope?" Helma asked Carter.

Ruth dropped back into her chair, her disappointed demeanor reverting to challenge, as if she were trying to, as TNT always said, "go another round." "Whoops. I forgot about that. So, did you?"

Carter shook his head. "The ring had been wiped clean and the lab didn't find anything usable on the paper, either."

"He wore gloves," Helma guessed. "I haven't told my mother yet that her ring's been recovered. May I return it to her?"

"Talk to the chief."

"I thought you were in charge, Carter," Ruth said, standing again.

"In the past," Carter said guardedly, his eyes narrowing at Helma, "there have been occasions when you kept vital details of an incident to yourself, to the detriment of a quick solution to a case. If you have any information that might help us, I expect you'll share it with us."

"You bet she will," Ruth said breezily.

Helma was shocked. She was being accused of uncooperativeness; being told she was *expected* to comply with someone else's misguided suspicions. "I always cooperate with the police," she informed him in her silver-dime voice. Carter didn't flinch.

"Especially now that she has a vested interest in the department's success," Ruth added.

At Carter's doorway, Ruth picked up a framed canvas that sat face-in to the wall and turned it to expose an oil painting. It was a sunset, approximately. At least the colors were sunset colors.

"Who did this?" Ruth held the painting at arm's length, critically eyeing it.

"It's a gift. I was thinking of hanging it, but..."

"'But' is right," Ruth agreed, gazing around Carter's tidy office. "It's nice, but I wouldn't call it your style." She set the painting down face-out and gave the frame a friendly pat. "I used to be a painter. Painted like the wind. Day and night. But then one day—poof – it was gone. All dried up. No more where that came from. I may as well turn my brushes into toothbrushes." She heaved a dramatic sigh. "Now I collect cat statues."

"I have to return to the library, Ruth," Helma said, leading the way from Carter's office into the hallway.

"See," Helma heard Ruth mumble behind her, "Everybody has something to do except me."

"Did you read your messages?" Glory Shandy asked, standing in the entrance to Helma's cubicle. Her face was bright in anticipation.

"Not yet," Helma told her, reaching for the pink slips that sat on her desk.

"He called. I took the message."

"He," in Glory's vernacular, usually meant Wayne Gallant, spoken in a breathy, reverent voice. Helma had completely dismissed from her mind Glory's duplicitous maneuvering for Wayne's attention two years earlier. Completely.

She picked up the three message slips on her desk, waiting for Glory to leave before she scanned them.

But Glory bit her lip and raised her shoulders to her ears like a child eager to divulge a surprise, who then expected a pat on the head for her cleverness. She couldn't wait for Helma to read the messages on her own. "It was Mr. Dubois," she blurted. "He's changed your appointment to tomorrow after work. He had a cancellation. He must need a head start on your transformation."

Then, Helma did scan her messages. The first one was from a book rep offering a special discount on the last-ever printed edition of the OED, the *Oxford English Dictionary*. And yes, the second one, in Glory Shandy's handwriting, which was beginning to resemble Ms. Moon's loopy cursive, related exactly what Glory had reported: Mr. Dubois had had a cancellation and would see her tomorrow evening after work. "Are you sure this is exactly what he said: a cancellation and tomorrow evening?" she asked Glory.

Glory's head bobbed and she held up her hand, arranging her fingers in a Brownie Scout pledge. "Exactly. Aren't you excited? He sounds so...foreign. I wonder what he'll do to you. He's probably very good at disguising mature skin."

"Thank you, Glory. I'll deal with my other messages now."

"Has he suggested another color besides white?" Glory went on. "White's not as flattering after thirty." She finally wandered off, musing, "Beige, probably."

Before Helma could read the third message, George Melville leaned over her cubicle wall. "Heard the latest?"

"I don't know," Helma said, "but if it's gossip I'm not interested."

"Nope. I saw it with my own eyes. Our rampaging local authors have uttered the deadly words 'law suit.'"

"I believe lawsuit is one word. On what grounds?"

"Unfair competition. One of them wandered inside and asked me to usher her to the legal section. She was throwing around testy phrases like 'restrictive practices,' 'monopolies' and 'local production.'"

"But the library's not *selling* the books," Helma pointed out, "only displaying them."

George shrugged. "All in the eyes of the beholder. Dutch said he saw the dead robber at the mission. Murder solved yet?"

"No. But the police are following several leads."

"They always say that when they don't have a clue."

Ms. Moon interrupted them, her face flushed and hands aflutter. "Excuse me, George, I must speak to Helma."

"Go ahead," George told her.

She cast one of her freezing glances at George until he raised his hands in surrender. "Okay, okay. I'm going."

"Helma, I hope you have a solution to this issue."

"I'm sorry?" Helma asked, wariness rising.

"The authors, of course." She waved toward the walls that faced the library's front doors where the authors presumably still picketed.

"Do you plan to have a staff meeting to discuss it?"

"That's not necessary. This issue naturally falls under your purview." She smiled benignly at Helma.

"In exactly what way?"

Ms. Moon leaned forward, her voice dropping to conspiratorial levels as if she and Helma were partners in a vital mission. "Glory reminded me that you were responsible for creating the Local Authors Collection. I'm sure you remember all the effort that went into that program?"

Sadly, Helma did, and the memory of the turmoil surrounding that collection made her briefly and unaccountably clench her teeth. "And?"

"These are local authors concerned about *their* books, so don't you agree it makes perfect sense for you to deal with them." She gazed at the ceiling. "You, after all, are...up to speed, that's it: up to speed, whereas I am totally, simply totally, consumed by our new library plans. It'll be so much more efficient this way."

"Are you giving me permission to tell them the display table of bestsellers will be abandoned?" Helma asked.

"Of course not," Ms. Moon said in honey tones, maintaining her smile but speaking with an undeniable edge to her voice. "The bestseller display is here to stay. There is no question of removing it."

"May I tell them there will be fewer multiple copies, then?"

"You may not."

"Then, what—" Helma began, but Ms. Moon raised her hand like a traffic director, stopping her.

"I have confidence you'll think of something. The bestseller display stays. Let me know when the authors go back home to... write," she finished, and gave a small wave, turning on her heel toward her office.

The Promise Mission for Homeless Men was located only a few blocks off Helma's route home. She drove her Buick into the small lot adjacent to the concrete building, forced to park uncomfortably close to a van covered with bumper stickers—actually one bumper sticker, repeated across its bumpers, doors, and sides, edge to edge. She wasn't tall enough to see if the roof was covered as well.

"For Every Long Journey there are Victims," every single bumper sticker read, white letters on a red background. In miniscule print, definitely too tiny to read from a following car, the sentiment was attributed to Napoleon. Apt, Helma thought, and resolved to look up the phrase's accuracy when she returned to the library.

Two men sprawled against the front steps of the mission, resting their elbows behind them, blurrily sharing a cigarette.

"Any change?" one of them asked her as she passed.

"No thank you," Helma told him.

Brother Danny sat at the reception desk, which was usually manned by one of the residents. The desk was covered with ledger sheets and what appeared to be receipts, many of them crumpled or folded.

"Miss Zukas," he drawled, rising to take her hand in his own thin hand, his smile broad. "Have you decided to come back to us?"

"Not yet," Helma said, recalling the unfair traffic ticket that had resulted in a community service sentence at the mission. "You're on the desk tonight?"

He nodded, explaining cheerfully: "Jack's sleeping off a bender. What can I do for you?"

The Promise Mission had been bought years ago with cash— "a valise full," she'd been told—by Brother Danny, and it ran on the force of his personality. Somehow, he managed to enforce strict—some claimed Draconian—rules and give the men a second chance, as he'd claimed he'd once been given. He inspired rabid devotion, yet he didn't hesitate to deal harshly with those who abused the second chance he offered.

"I don't expect you to divulge privileged information," Helma began.

"You asking about Chip Block, too?" he asked her. He came around the desk and she noticed he was even thinner than she remembered.

"Has someone else?"

He nodded toward the door at the same time he held out a box of tissues to a man hacking into his bare hands. Helma clasped her own hands behind her back. "Police just left not five minutes ago. That straight-up-and-down detective."

"Carter Houston," Helma said, thinking she was right: Carter *hadn't* known Chip Block had spent the night at the mission. Surely the glint she'd spotted in Carter's eyes hadn't been evidence of competition with Ruth? Not Carter?

"The very man. Wanted to know if I remembered him."

"Do you?"

Brother Danny nodded sadly. "And now he's dead. Sorry to hear it, but I'm not so surprised."

"Did he cause trouble here?"

"Nothing unusual, but he struck me as a man who'd made a few important mistakes. I heard he was noising it around he was looking for a way to make money."

"You aren't speaking of a legitimate job?"

"Brother Danny smiled. "Doubt it."

"He must have connected with someone, either here or on the street." Helma couldn't see how else a stranger would end up robbing her mother and Aunt Em, unless he was tipped to it by another unsavory person. "Did you see who?"

"Like I told your cop, I didn't see him involved in any suspicious exchanges, but it could have happened out of my sight, easy."

"He arrived alone, then?" Helma asked.

The two men who'd been smoking outside entered the building and leaned against the lobby wall, watching. "Chips and cola in the chapel, gentlemen," Brother Danny told them, and they wandered toward the chapel that also served as classroom, basketball court and overflow sleeping quarters.

"He was alone here," Brother Danny told her. "Don't know what happened after he left. He only spent the one night he had left to him with us."

Helma thanked him, and Brother Danny walked her to the door and reached out his hand to shake hers. "The dining room has never run as well as when you were here. You ever get tired of librarying, there's always a place for you here."

Helma laughed, surprised by a sharp little glow of pride.

TNT was opening the door of his Jeep when Helma pulled her Buick into the car port. She almost didn't recognize him. He shone in a gray suit and striped blue tie, and carried a bouquet of daisies. His face was pink from a fresh shave.

"Off to your mother's and aunt's," he said over a dry rasp in his throat. "You think she'll like these?" He held up the flowers.

"She'll love them," Helma assured him. "You look very handsome."

"I'm as nervous as a spotty boy about to meet his first date's parents."

"Aunt Em's made you a special Lithuanian potato dish," Helma advised him. "Ask for second helpings and you'll win her heart,"

He relaxed. "Ah, potatoes is it? Then I'm in."

She studied the bank of mailboxes at the foot of the stairs to her apartment as she approached them. She couldn't help it; she glanced over both shoulders, then toward the corners of her building, eyes sharp for anyone watching. Someone who might have slipped her mother's ring into her mailbox. And who might have deposited another surprise for her.

The mailboxes weren't locked. Bellehaven was no longer a small town, and it was time for the owner to order an upgrade. She bent down and peered carefully inside her mail cubby before pulling out an ordinary stack of envelopes and circulars.

Boy Cat Zukas wasn't in his usual spot on Helma's balcony. After sorting her mail into Toss and Keep, grateful not to discover any mysterious letters or packages, she opened her balcony door anyway in case the cat was sitting on TNT's balcony or hulking on the roof, but when he didn't appear after thirty seconds, she closed it. There were times when he stayed out overnight and slept languorously for hours after his return, despite her best efforts to encourage regular hours.

Following a light dinner of spinach salad and a slice of roast chicken—no skin—Helma stacked her dishes and sat at her table, reflecting on Ruth's plan to meet the blond man at Joker's that evening. Ruth had said seven o'clock. She was as likely to be early as late. But the odds were more likely she'd be late.

If the blond man was interested in Ruth—and many younger men were—it was likely he would be the earlier arrival. As she considered her options, Helma washed her dinner dishes in her double sink. She'd never used the dishwasher in her apartment and was sure that by now its gears had rusted and its seals withered. It made a perfect storage unit for odorous cat food and treats.

She was interrupted by two strident jabs of her doorbell, and when she peered through the peephole, she recognized the distorted face of Walter David, the Bayside Arms manager.

"Is Moggy here?" he demanded as Helma opened the door. His eyes were wide and frantic; he nervously shifted, peering over Helma's shoulder into her kitchen. "On your balcony?"

"I haven't seen her," Helma told him. "Come in. You can check yourself."

He entered, his eyes anxiously sweeping around her apartment.

"I know she's not inside my apartment," Helma assured him. "What happened?"

She removed the safety stick and unlocked the sliding glass doors for him. He brushed past her and in jittery, abrupt movements, checked behind her flower pots, along the railings, even leaning back and inspecting the roof overhang.

"We were practicing for the show and Mrs. Pinkney's poodle..." He spluttered and couldn't finish. "Moggy ran around the corner of the building and was gone by the time I got there, just vanished. She's never been an outside cat; she doesn't have a clue how to behave in the wild."

"Does she have her claws?" Helma asked.

"Of course. She's a purebred." He turned back to Helma. "Where's that cat of yours?"

Helma couldn't help it; she bristled a little at the term "that cat." "Boy Cat Zukas hasn't returned from his daily outing yet."

"He hangs around my patio sometimes," he said suspiciously. Walter David lived on the ground floor and had constructed a mock split rail fence around his balcony-sized patio.

"Boy Cat Zukas was neutered years ago," she said. She didn't remind Walter that it had been Moggy's fault that Boy Cat Zukas had undergone the knife. His unrepentant tom-cattedness hadn't bothered Helma. "I'm certain he has nothing to do with Moggy's disappearance."

Walter shuddered when she uttered the word "disappearance," and Helma hastily added, "If she's unaccustomed to the outside, she's likely hiding beneath a bush." She imagined the flat-faced Persian with its doll-like eyes and hoped it actually did have sense enough to head for a restricted space. "Have you looked beneath the cars in the parking lot?"

He shook his head. "I'll do that now. Let me know if you see her, would you?"

"I'll contact you immediately," Helma promised.

After Walter left, Helma checked her balcony and the roof, just as Walter had. There was no sign of Boy Cat Zukas.

CHAPTER 13

Jokers Wild

Helma left her apartment at 6:39, hearing in the distance, Walter David calling, "Moggy? Here, kitty, kitty, kitty," joined by Jaynie Lynn's "Moggy, Moggy," supplemented by a sing-song of credible purring sounds, and drove to Joker's, originally a rough, fishermen's and dock workers' bar that had gone through so many permutations it had inevitably migrated to upscale, where the once-useful tools of the fishermen and stevedores hung on the walls as ornamentation. Joker's was situated close to the shore, and the smell of salt water, decaying seaweed, and dead fish only added spice to its presumed authenticity.

She parked her Buick at the edge of the rough gravel lot so she could watch the front door, but far enough away that her car had less chance of being bumped. She'd recognize the blond man, she was sure, but at 6:52, when he still hadn't appeared, she began to suspect he'd arrived before her and was already inside. The shadowy outline of a man smoking shifted near the rear parking lot of Joker's, but he was too bulky to be the tall, slender man she was looking for. She sighed and stepped out of her car, feeling the moist air against her cheek.

The sun hadn't set yet. Joker's only window was the glass panel decorating the wooden entrance door. Inside, it felt like evening: shadowy dark wood walls and deep green trim. A rectangular mirror backed the bar that was likely more ornate than the original. She knew Kipper, the bartender, and he nodded to her, just as if she were a regular.

She spotted the blond man at once. He sat at the bar, his long legs wrapped around a bar stool, alone, positioned so he could watch the front door. His eyes passed over Helma without really seeing her. He appeared far too young to patronize Joker's, and she wondered if Kipper had adequately checked his ID before serving the beer in front of him.

Helma chose the stool one removed from the blond man and sat down, carefully positioning her purse on her lap and looping the strap around her wrist. Kipper raised his eyebrows at her. "A…" She looked at the bottle in front of the blond man and finished, "Sleeman Honey Brown."

The beery fragrance that permeated Joker's conjured an old image of her father and uncles engaged in one of their raucous card games, drinking hot beer with butter and sour cream stirred into it.

She didn't like beer any better than she liked coffee, but she also believed in setting a scene for comfort, particularly when one planned to conduct a subtle interrogation. This was not the moment to request tea. The blond man didn't look at her.

Helma had once assisted a library patron in finding information on the proper way to pour beer, and when Kipper delivered the bottle and glass to her, she tipped her glass and poured from the bottle so that only bubbles formed on the amber liquid's surface, not foam.

The blond man glanced at her glass but didn't raise his eyes to hers. Helma seized the moment.

"I believe I assisted your father with the Russian Revolution today," she said to him, her lips forming a friendly smile. "In the library."

His brow wrinkled, but no recognition lit his eyes. "Everett?" he said, and Helma stored that name away. "No relation. I just give him rides sometimes."

"After he left, I thought of a few more sources for him."

"He'll be back," he said shortly, glancing again toward the door.

"Is the Russian revolution an interest of yours, too?"

"Nope," he said, and Helma felt herself being dismissed, sensed he was about to pick up his bottle and glass and move farther down the bar, or to a table. She glanced at her watch. It was precisely seven o'clock. Ruth would arrive any moment and Helma's chance would be lost.

"What did you give my Aunt Emily this morning?" she asked him. "In the pink shoebox?"

Finally, he focused totally on Helma, stroking his inadequate wisp of a beard. "Huh?"

"At the Silver Gables," Helma clarified. "She gave you an envelope, which I presume held money and you gave her a pink shoebox. What was inside?"

He appraised her, his blue eyes cool. "Did you ask her?"

"She has memory difficulties."

He shrugged. "Not my problem."

"Of course it isn't," Helma agreed, pausing before she said, "Perhaps I could ask someone with more experience in the art of cross examination to question her about the exchange I witnessed." She paused. "Or even search her apartment."

"You a cop?" He reared back from her, as far as his barstool would allow.

"No, I'm a librarian, an employee of the City of Bellehaven, the same as the police." It was a mistake that she hadn't asked him sooner, before she'd challenged him, but she tried anyway. "I'm Miss Helma Zukas, and you are...?"

He tipped his head and just as she expected, he didn't answer.

"It wasn't illegal," he said, "if that's what you're thinking."

"Then why was the exchange so clandestine?"

"Look. Your aunt wanted 999, and I could get it for her. Sure, she paid for it, but there's no other way to get it, is there?"

Before Helma could ask him to explain "999," Ruth stood between them. "What's going on?" she asked, turning her head from Helma to the blond man. She wore nearly normal clothes: black pants with tall boots, a blue and red sweater that hung to her thighs and her hair actually tamed into a low tail, her Bride of Frankenstein streak contained.

The blond man's face flushed. "Is this a setup?"

"I don't know," Ruth answered, looking at Helma. "You tell me. Is it?"

"Of course not. I was just..."

The man stood. "Well, I'm not interested in whatever you two are peddling," and he stomped out of Joker's, banging the door behind him.

"Oh shit," Ruth slumped onto the blond man's barstool. "What did you do, Helma?" She picked up his glass and drained the remaining beer.

"Nothing. I recognized him, that's all. I was simply establishing a connection."

"While you just happened to be hanging out here in the bar, you mean? On one of your little weeknights on the town? Come on, you never go to bars alone, Helma Zukas."

"I saw him deliver a box to Aunt Em this morning," she said, hoping to divert Ruth from inquiries into bar-hopping. She slid her untouched glass of beer toward Ruth as an added incentive. "Are you sure you didn't get his name in the library?"

"Names never came up. So what was in the box?" Ruth reached for Helma's beer.

"Something called 999. Do you know what that is?"

"Never heard of it. Ask your aunt."

"She claimed she doesn't remember any delivery."

"And you don't believe her."

"No." At one time in her life Helma wouldn't have doubted a single word Aunt Em said; a "brain incident" had changed all that, exposing Aunt Em's shocking past and a side of her Helma had never dreamed existed.

Ruth nodded toward the door of Joker's. "There went yet another chance for love. Out the window, thanks to you."

"Out the door," Helma corrected. "He was too young for you, anyway," she pointed out."

"I'm wounded. Age is immaterial." Her shoulders hunched. "He could have been a pleasant diversion. There's not much in my life that interests me right now, know what I mean?"

"Because a man you spoke to for a few minutes in the library and whose name you don't even know, has walked out the door without...engaging with you?" Helma couldn't keep the incredulity from her voice.

"That's only what it looks like to you. It's cumulative: no art, no man to provide human interaction, no income, nada." She poured more beer into her glass—incorrectly, and created three inches of foam. Her words were light, but Ruth's dejection was serious and trending downward. How many times had Helma heard Ruth announce her recipe for overcoming depression, "Let yourself sink into the blackest hole until there's nothing left to do but to rise back to the surface."

Ruth was definitely sinking. Their reflection looked back from the mirror behind the bar. Ruth's eyes were unfocused, inward. Helma swiveled her bar stool slightly toward Ruth. "I wish I knew how to keep my mother from turning this wedding into a carnival,"

Ruth raised her head and turned her foamy beer glass between her palms. "Give up. She's going to strike up the band and bring in the dancing elephants whether you want her to or not."

"I suppose," Helma said. "I'm afraid it won't feel like my own if she's too involved."

Yes, Helma had made the statement in an attempt to distract Ruth from herself, but once she'd voiced it, she recognized
the truth. Helma had only seen one of her mother's computer
files—so far—but she'd noted the stack of bridal magazines, the
yellow pages open to caterers, and the swatches of colors. There
was Mr. Dubois. And Lillian had only known of Helma's engagement for two days. Project that into months…

If her mother persisted, the only aspect Helma would have
control over was how fast she walked down the aisle. Every other
matter would be a battle, or at least a skirmish leading to pain
and injury.

Ruth looked at her now, one corner of her mouth raised.
"Maybe I can help calm her down a little."

Helma didn't dare think what that might entail, but she
said, with true gratitude, "Is that a possibility?"

"Sure. Trust me."

The sky hung black over Washington Bay when Helma
returned to the Bayside Arms. As she crossed the parking lot
from the carport she noted there were neither stars nor moon
visible over the dark water, signifying another cloudy "mizzley"
night. To the north, Bellehaven's lights formed a miasma of shine
so dense it appeared solid.

Walter David's lights shone from the windows of his apartment, his curtains open, and the manager himself sat on a kitchen
chair in front of his door. He raised a hand toward Helma and
she detoured around the stairs to greet him.

"Moggy hasn't returned yet?" she asked him. On his lap he
held the lamb's wool pad that normally hung over the back of his
sofa, where Moggy reclined, staring out at the world.

Walter shook his head. "Not yet," he said forlornly, absently
stroking the lamb's wool. "She's a valuable cat. If somebody stole
her…" His voice caught and he looked away from Helma.

"She's too frightened to leave her hiding place now that it's dark," Helma assured him, hoping that was true. "She'll be here in the morning."

"All night," Walter mused. "She's never been out all night before. I don't even let her go outside by herself."

Helma said nothing more about Moggy, suspecting a night-time experience would be beneficial for every animal. But she did remember the other subject she hadn't broached with Walter earlier because he'd been so distracted.

"Did you notice a stranger near the mailboxes Sunday evening or during the day on Monday?"

Walter's brow creased, forming shadows across his forehead. "Near the mailboxes?" he repeated. "Sunday or Monday?"

"Yes. Not the mailman, but a person placing an unauthorized envelope into my mailbox?"

"No, I didn't see anyone like that," Walter told her, exhibiting an unusual lack of interest in events at the Bayside Arms.

"I *did* see your mother," he said.

"Here?"

"She arrived a little while ago, with TNT." He nodded upward toward TNT's apartment next to her own. His windows were dark, curtains closed.

"She left already?" Helma asked, and immediately regretted it because in the darkness she detected the embarrassed grimace on Walter's face.

"I haven't seen her," he said, and hastily added, "Thanks for keeping an eye out for Moggy. I'll phone you if I find her."

"*When* you find her," Helma amended. "Goodnight."

Helma didn't actually pause outside TNT's apartment; she merely slowed her steps because she was approaching her own apartment. Yes, the curtains were closed, but not tightly. TNT's living room behind the gap was dark, not even the television cast its flickering light.

Inside her own apartment, Helma removed her coat and immediately crossed the room to the sliding glass doors onto her balcony. She didn't turn on the outside light and quietly removed the safety stick. She was not sneaking, definitely not. Moggy might be hiding on her balcony and naturally she didn't want to scare the cat away.

She slowly slid open the glass door and stepped into the night. A breeze ruffled her hair. On the wood decking of the balcony, her crepe soles were silent. She moved to the railing closest to TNT's apartment.

His apartment was dark on this side of the building as well, these curtains also closed. No sounds. Perhaps her mother had left and Walter had missed seeing her, too distracted by his search for Moggy.

A faint yellow light flickered behind the curtains. A candle? She watched for a few seconds. Yes, a candle.

She politely turned her back on all that was contained in TNT's apartment and recrossed her balcony, certainly minding her own business. She stepped through her doorway and was about to close the door when she noticed Boy Cat Zukas sitting in the shadows on the opposite railing, not moving, not attempting to squeeze past her, watching her in mild feline interest.

She stood in the open door, expecting him to leap down and follow her inside. When he didn't, she began sliding closed the door. He didn't move. The glass door was two inches from the jamb when a squeak sounded. Boy Cat Zukas blinked. He was not a squeaking type of cat. She looked down, and next to the door, lying against the white siding of her balcony wall was what she first perceived to be a wet towel.

The squeak sounded again and Helma switched on her outside light. The dirty towel was Moggy: filthy, matted, all the cat's fluffiness gone as flat as if it had been dunked in a tub of water. The cat was too miserable to even lift its head to gaze up at Helma. Its round eyes were closed.

Moggy was in a most unappealing state, rather rattish-looking, actually. Helma glanced back at Boy Cat Zukas, who still hadn't even flinched, suspicious that somehow he was responsible for Moggy's condition. Helma Zukas did not converse with animals nor touch cats, but she retrieved an old towel from her bathroom and laid it on the floor before she opened her balcony door wider.

That done, she phoned Walter David.

"Yes?" he answered. Breathless.

"It's Helma. Your cat is on my balcony. It's—"

"I'm on my way," and the phone banged down. Less than ten seconds later she heard Walter's footsteps pounding up the staircase. Moggy still hadn't ventured inside. Helma opened her door and Walter ran — actually ran - across the room and dove through her balcony door, swooping up the sopping cat.

"You can take the towel," Helma told him as he crooned and rocked Moggy.

"How can I ever thank you?" While ministering to his cat, Walter glanced around her apartment. "Where's Boy Cat Zukas?"

She heard the touch of suspicion in his voice. She had no reason to shield Boy Cat Zukas, but she flicked off her balcony light. "I don't see him," she said, peering out onto the dark balcony.

CHAPTER 14

Numbers Matter

The previous year, Helma had finally—"I think you're the last in the country," Ruth had said—after meticulous research and returning two, become the owner of a personal computer. She worked on computers the majority of her days at the library, and the last thing she wanted was to sit in front of one at home. Her computer was as much unlike her work computer as possible: a laptop with all available options and maximum memory so it hopefully wouldn't be obsolete in six months.

After Boy Cat Zukas finally entered her apartment with a switch of his tail and retreated to his basket without eating, she opened her computer and performed a search for the mysterious 999 the blond man had claimed he'd given Aunt Em because "she wanted it and he could get it for her."

She cast a wide net, first entering simply "999" in her search engine, which garnered 150 million hits. She began paging through them. Radio frequency, casinos, punk bands, art movements. She paused at a Chinese herbal medicine and then went on to addresses and telephone numbers, predictions of doom, and song lyrics.

After skimming twelve pages, she sat back, blinked her eyes and performed a series of shoulder stretches she'd learned from a city-provided book titled *Get Off Your Back*. Perhaps he hadn't said 999; it had only sounded like the number 999. But Helma was thorough. She left the number in the search field and began adding elements of Aunt Em, perhaps something she might desire that Lillian or Helma couldn't get her? But something a sullen young man could?

Aunt Em wouldn't touch illegal drugs, would she? "999" and "drugs" informed her that 999 was the UK's equivalent to 911. The blond man had said there was no other way to procure 999 except through him, so it had to be something not available locally. She added the word, "imported" and brought up pages of oddly named cars with the numbers 999 in their prices.

Next, she added the word "alcohol" to 999 and thanks to the miracle of bits and bytes and instant access-to-it-all communication, there it was in plain sight before her eyes at the top of the first page:

999, the most famous alcoholic drink in Lithuania.

She sat back, even swiveled her office chair. Of course! How had she missed it? 999 equaled three nines, or the name she had known it by: *trejos devynerios*: three nines, for the double-digit list of ingredients. Her grandmother had brewed a version of it called *Krupnikas*. Probably at one time, her father and his brothers had, too, and Aunt Em, also. It was potent, containing a mix of herbs and grain alcohol enveloped in a nearly sacred aura. Medicinal, favorite motivator of the great Vytautas before battle, mood enhancer, health restorer, and who knew what other touted benefits.

Helma had seen the worn recipe on Aunt Em's counter when she was a girl, its list of herbs and spices tempered with the helpful admonition, "Do not let explode."

999 wasn't available in the United States. It wasn't imported. It came from Kaunas, the second largest city in Lithuania, and could only enter the United States with someone who'd personally visited Lithuania.

She should have recognized it immediately. Aunt Em had been nostalgic for the old drink and had found a person who would procure it for her.

And that "who" was obvious: someone connected to her Lithuanian club.

CHAPTER 15

Morning Surprises

The next morning Helma was careful not to make any undue noise as she prepared for work. She shooed Boy Cat Zukas out the door on the street side of the building rather than opening her sliding glass doors. Her shower was abnormally brief, and she skipped watching the morning news on television.

All accomplished in the name of being considerate of her neighbors.

She stepped outside, quietly closing and relocking her door, and picked up the morning's *Bellehaven Daily News* that lay on her doormat, tucking it beneath her arm to peruse at the library.

It was another misty morning, but there were subtleties to mist, from the dark silent mists that portended rain, to the silvery mist like this morning that would burn off by noon, allowing a few rays of sunshine that were sometimes so potent it tricked Bellehavenites into believing they'd just lived through a sunny day. A bicyclist whirred past, emerging from hazy air as Helma watched, and disappearing again in a slow fade.

As she turned to walk from her apartment down the stairs and across the lot to the car ports where her Buick waited, the door of TNT's apartment swung open, and TNT, barefoot and wearing a white terrycloth robe, reached out to pick up his newspaper. Helma froze, pausing to give him time to slip back inside and close his door.

It was not to be. He raised his head, his fingers still on the paper, and saw Helma. His mouth opened, then closed and opened again. He flushed brilliant red. His iron gray hair reflected his blush, taking on a pinkish cast. He rose, clutching his robe tightly closed with one thick fist.

"Ah, good morning to ye. Aye, good morning." He bobbed his head.

Helma nodded and moved closer to the railing to pass around him. And as she did, a shriek emitted from inside his apartment. "Oh, Helma. Oh my. Good morning, dear."

What else could she do, but halt and acknowledge the situation. Through TNT's open door, she could see that her mother, also barefoot, wore one of TNT's sweatshirts that hemmed her at bare mid-thigh. She stood at his counter, interrupted while pouring coffee into two mismatched mugs.

"Good morning, Mother, TNT."

TNT, his red face fading to pink, beckoned her inside, saying. "My intentions toward your mother are honorable, Helma. I swear it."

It wasn't as if Helma hadn't known, it was just that this was the first time she'd been confronted by irrefutable evidence. "And what are those intentions?" she asked TNT, sounding even to herself like a shocked parent.

"Well, your mother and I... last night...We've decided..." The tough boxer, the self-proclaimed TNT—Dynamite Man, stuttered, ran down, and looked beseechingly at Lillian.

"I'm moving in," Lillian said calmly, dropping two sugar cubes into her own mug and pouring a splash of skim milk into TNT's.

"Here?" Helma asked helplessly. "Next door?"

"This is where TNT lives," her mother said, speaking as if Helma hadn't noticed.

"What about Aunt Em?"

Lillian left the counter and stepped closer to Helma. Her face softened and she ran a hand through her tangled hair. "Em wants to move to the second floor." She looked into Helma's eyes as if it were Helma she was worried about. "Em's been talking about it for a while."

"The second floor," Helma repeated. "Aunt Em wants to move to the second floor?"

Lillian nodded, leaning forward and touching Helma's shoulder.

The second floor of the Silver Gables was reserved for residents who needed more...assistance, who might have memory problems or mobility issues. Helma swallowed. "When?"

"Not right away. This is Em's decision and it'll happen when she's ready, not before." She smiled past Helma at TNT. "And that's when I'll move in here."

"I asked her to marry me," TNT blurted.

"I've been married," Lillian said.

"You're going to live together?" Helma asked.

"Is that embarrassing to you, dear?"

"I asked her to marry me," TNT repeated, his jaw set.

"It's a surprise," Helma finally admitted, watching her mother place TNT's black coffee mug in his hand.

"You'll get over it." Her mother's attention shifted to TNT, a secret smile passing between them, TNT flushing again.

Helma left TNT's apartment, and it wasn't until she was pulling out of her car port that she realized her mother hadn't once mentioned Helma's future marriage or the robbery.

On the stairwell's second floor landing in the Silver Gables, Helma noted the blink of the new security camera mounted near the ceiling. She resisted the sudden surprising urge to wave.

Aunt Em was awake, dressed, and sitting at the table with a plate of leftover *kugelis* and the morning's newspaper folded flat on the table to the obituaries. Her eyes were sharp and clear; it was a "good" morning. "Find yourself a plate," Aunt Em told her, pointing her fork toward the cupboard.

"I saw Mother at TNT's this morning," Helma told her as she sat down across from her.

Aunt Em dabbed at her mouth with her napkin. "She and that old boxer had bees in their pants to leave last night. Like kids. At least he knows good food," and she pointed her fork at her plate.

"She said she's going to live with TNT."

Aunt Em nodded and cut off a piece of *kugelis* and slid it onto Helma's plate. "They have to before they're too old."

"Do you really want to move to the second floor, Aunt Em?"

She patted Helma's hand. "I didn't think about it for years. And then one day, it was time. Life is like that. You're not ready and then without making up your mind, you are. So now I'm ready."

"You could come live with Wayne and me when we're married."

Aunt Em laughed. "No thank you. I am better inside my own walls."

"When do you plan to move? Have you talked to the manager yet?" She savored the mealy potato dish, thinking that yes, there was room in any diet for bacon grease.

"Do not worry, Wilhelmina. When everything is ready, it will happen. Did you take my card to the Lithuanian club?"

"I did," Helma told her as if she hadn't already told her twice before, because now she had another reason to bring up the Lithuanian Club. "I gave it to Dalia Stone."

"*Stoniene*," Aunt Em corrected, turning the simple surname into Lithuanian. "Dalia is a married lady."

"Is she the person who gave you the 999?" Helma asked, keeping her voice casual, as if she and her aunt had discussed the healthful benefits of 999 in conversation multiple times already.

Aunt Em shook her head just as casually. "No, she did not."

"Then who did? Who was the man who gave it to you? The man with the pink box?"

"Are you going to turn him in to the police?"

"Was he doing something illegal?" Helma asked, and Aunt Em shook her head, glancing away.

"How much did you pay him?"

"Too much, just like I expected. So is okay."

"But, Aunt Em..."

"Is okay," she repeated. Her mouth closed in that straight tight-lipped line Helma had seen on her own father's face: subject closed.

"Wayne wonders if you recall anything new about the robbery," she tried. "The police are still looking for the other robber."

"And my *Stelmužė* box?"

"Yes." She paused "What was inside the box, Aunt Em?"

"My Papa carved it," she said, and again, that tight-lipped line. She tapped the page of obituaries folded in front of her. "Did you read this one? It says he played the piano in front of Queen Elizabeth. Think of that."

"Have you talked to them yet?"

Helma raised her eyes from the blue bag she'd just dropped on her desk and met Glory's wide eyes, framed by fluttering lashes. "Whom?"

"The striking authors."

"They're not really on strike, Glory. That would mean they'd quit writing."

Glory frowned. "If they did that, they wouldn't be authors anymore."

"Technically," Helma agreed.

She'd entered the workroom through the door on the loading dock, but she'd seen the local authors on the front sidewalk,

drinking coffee from paper cups and insulated mugs, their placards at rest by their feet. The morning was still cool, and most
wore jackets, a few sported knit caps. They'd stood ominously
silent, gazing at the library's front doors as if awaiting solemn
news.

"Ms. Moon said you're taking care of it," Glory went on, "so
they're going to be really mad at you."

"I'm sure the situation can be resolved."

"How? Ms. Moon won't give up the bestseller table. It's going
to be just awful, especially for you."

"Excuse me. I have work to do."

"Are you sick again?"

Helma disregarded the irritated buzzing beginning at the
back of her neck. She removed her heels from her bag and that's
when she noticed the white cardboard box sitting on her desk,
addressed to her.

"Excuse me," she said to Glory again and waited for her to
leave, then placed her bag in the lower drawer of her desk and
buttoned her coat on its hanger before she turned her attention
to the white box.

It was one of the Post Office's "If it fits, it ships" boxes: a
small one. There was no return address and her name had been
printed and affixed using a stick-on label, not handwritten. She
cautiously nudged the box to one corner of her desk, remembering her mother's wedding ring. Maybe this time she really should
call the police?

No, her mother's wedding ring had been delivered to her
apartment, not the library. This was entirely different: ordered
library materials, a gift from a library patron grateful for library
service. Hadn't she once received a box of Godiva chocolates from
a woman she'd helped win a wager with her new husband over
latex sensitivity? They may have forgotten to include their return
address. But still…

She left the box untouched while she served her time on the reference desk, which was punctuated by a boy in his early teens sitting a few tables away wearing earbuds and who kept breaking into an off-key warble. His body moved to unheard music as if he had no bones.

Forty-five minutes into her reference stint, the boy removed his ear pieces, pulled on a khaki stocking cap, and approached the desk.

"How may I help you?" Helma asked.

"My mom's supposed to pick me up at ten forty-five." He swung his earbuds like a lariat.

"Yes?" she asked, uncertain what he needed.

"So what time is it now?"

Helma never turned away a library patron's question, no matter its legitimacy, without providing some type of positive assistance, but there were questions that answered themselves. The boy faced the clock that hung on the wall behind her left shoulder. Perhaps he had vision challenges.

"Is this clock difficult for you to see?" she asked, but kindly.

He shook his head. "I see it, but it's the wrong kind of clock."

Helma turned to look at the classic round wall clock with its oversized numbers and sweeping hands, even a faintly ticking second hand.

"Do you mean because it's an analog clock and not a digital clock?"

He was unembarrassed. "Yeah, I can't read those old-fashioned clocks."

It was, as Ms. Moon sometimes said, a "teaching moment." Helma considered the boy's irritated, impatient stance. No, she decided, it wasn't.

"The time is exactly ten forty-five," she told him, and watched as he turned on his heel and left before she'd completed her sentence.

Dalia Stone's name wasn't listed in the Bellehaven telephone book, although one of the listings read "J and D Stone," and she guessed that might be her number. There were eight other Stones in the Bellehaven area and none of the names began with a D.

A woman's cell phone fell from her purse and Helma raised her head at the clatter, glancing toward the magazine racks where the blond man had talked to Ruth and waited for Everett. It wasn't too late to look up the name of the man who'd checked out the Russian Revolution books. Helma watched the woman return her cell phone to her purse. She swallowed. No. Not now, not ever.

At the end of her reference desk shift, Harley arrived to replace her. He approached with his head held high, barely moving his mouth as he spoke. His face was curiously expressionless.

As he set his stack of papers on the desktop, she noticed the uppermost article was an internet printout titled: "Botox Side Effects."

Helma returned to her cubicle and without further vacillation—and with no further thought of phoning the police—used her letter opener to open the small package. It would be foolish to imply she held it away from her body as she slit the tape and pulled up the flaps, although she did pay attention.

No note. Layers of plastic bubble wrap had been taped around the object inside so it fit snugly into the cardboard box. From the shape and heft of the package, she wasn't surprised to finish unwinding the bubble wrap and discover Aunt Em's precious *Stelmužė* box. It lay against the silvery plastic, its delicate geometric designs carved into every surface, top and bottom and sides.

She gazed at it for several moments, appreciating her grandfather's artistic skill. The box's intricate patterns were common to Lithuanian tapestries: symmetrical, with stylized motifs that from one angle appeared to be flowers and from another, something quite different, even faces.

She remembered her grandfather as a straight-backed figure in black boots. He'd kept horses on his farm for years after every other farmer had moved on to machinery. "He understood good horseflesh better than he did farming," she'd heard her father say.

Library workroom noise swirled around her: key tapping, low voices, the scritch of unfurling tape as new book covers were applied. She reached her hand toward the telephone, then pulled it back. The police still had her mother's wedding ring. Her mother wasn't aware Helma had discovered it in her mailbox, and Carter hadn't told Helma *when* it would be returned to her.

She couldn't allow Aunt Em's *Stelmužė* box to drop into police oblivion. Before she rewrapped the package, she lifted the box and examined it, turning it in her hands, side to side, top to bottom. It was carved from golden, tight-grained oak, heavy in her hands, and definitely appeared to be a box, but it was solid, without give, or any scoring to indicate where it might open: only a complex pattern of lines and angles.

She ran her fingers over its surface, feeling its intricate geometry beneath her fingertips, searching for a latch or hinge, some way to open it. Nothing. She shook it, alert to a rattle or a shifting of contents. Again, nothing.

Aunt Em's *Stelmužė* box was a solid block of carved wood, perhaps carved so intricately by her grandfather to counteract boredom during Lithuania's long winter months.

She carried the box in her purse to the Silver Gables during her lunch hour, forgetting as she opened the front door of the library, the picketing authors. She rarely retreated once she'd set her path, and now she nodded to the encircling authors, calling a few by name, Rob, the mystery writer, Erik the science fiction author, and Angi who wrote novels for teens,

"Are you going to fix this?" Margaret, a poet Helma recognized, asked.

"Yes, we will," she assured the poet in a firm and positive voice, confident that without a doubt, somehow, *she* would.

"Your mother isn't home yet," Aunt Em told her, shaking her head. "I hope they don't give each other heart attacks."

"I have something for you, Aunt Em," she said, unwrapping the carved box and setting it on the table in front of her aunt.

Aunt Em clasped her hands to her face. Tears filled her eyes and spilled down, shimmering in the creases of her cheeks. "Oh, Wilhelmina, you found it. I'm so happy." She held out her hands and Helma gently placed the *Stelmužė* box in her cupped palms. She cradled it to her heart, whispering words Helma didn't understand. Helma looked away.

Finally Aunt Em wiped her eyes. "Did your policeman find it? Where was it?"

"It was sent to me, but I don't know who sent it."

"The robber knew what it meant and felt guilty," she said with a tone of certainty.

"What *does* it mean?" Helma asked her.

"Nothing special to any person but me." Aunt Em set the box on the table in front of her and gazed at it. Tears gathered once again in her eyes.

Helma touched her arm and asked, "How did the robber know how much it meant to you, then?"

A crafty look passed through Aunt Em's eyes, as if she'd realized she'd said something to give herself away. "He guessed."

"Aunt Em, did you *know* the robber?"

Aunt Em vigorously shook her head. "No, no. I do not," she insisted.

"I read about the ancient oak in Stelmužė. It's in the northern area of the country, close to Latvia. That's a long way from where you were born. Did grandfather travel to Stelmužė for the wood?"

Aunt Em shrugged. "Who is to know? That time is gone, rain into rivers."

"Aunt Em, is there a man at the Lithuanian club named Everett? A gentleman interested in the Russian Revolution?"

"The Russian Revolution? That was before I was a baby. I have to go to the bathroom, Wilhelmina. Help me up."

Helma did, but then Aunt Em waved her away as she tried to help her down the hallway. "I can still walk to do my own business," she said.

Helma returned to the dining room and realized her mother's laptop computer sat on the table with its cover open and the screen black. She nudged it and a screen saver of deep woods came to life, fading in and out at the screen's edges in a Ken Burns effect.

Her mother had been gone for at least eighteen hours; the computer should have turned itself off long ago. She glanced down the hallway: Aunt Em had been using the computer? She couldn't picture it, not with her gnarled hands and faulty eyesight.

Helma touched the computer mouse lightly with one finger and the screensaver disappeared, exposing a list of her mother's files. She scanned them, all in alphabetical order: Emily's Health, Gin and Rummy Club, Grandchildren, shuddered over a file titled "Helma and Wayne's wedding," Lithuanian Club, Silver Gables Robbery.

She wondered if Aunt Em had been trying to read the file about herself: "Emily's Health." She stared at the file name, then the blinking curser. There might be a way she could help interpret the information. Was Aunt Em's condition serious enough she *really* needed to move to the second floor? If Lillian had been present, Helma certainly would have asked her for permission to open the file. But who knew when her mother would return.

One swift click and the spreadsheet titled Emily's Health bared itself in front of her. She recognized a few of the medications: Lisinopril, Coumadin, Lipitor, and in the spiral notebook she always carried with her, she jotted down the names of the others.

Aunt Em's blood pressure was noted, her weight for each doctor's visit, and Lillian had developed a code system for her state of mind every day: The letters G, M, or P under a column titled, "Memory." Good, Medium, or Poor, Helma guessed. There were several Ps, more in recent days.

The final column read "Oddities," and listed under it were brief accounts, such as "Robbery, dead man," or comments about Aunt Em's behavior, including: "Fell asleep during 'Dancing with the Stars,'" followed by two explanation points as if that one were a shockingly noteworthy development. Another note read "Forgot how she liked her coffee," and "Called me Tofelia," Aunt Em's dead sister.

She closed the file and peered again at the list, the folder titled "Lithuanian Club" jumping out at her. Why hadn't she thought of it sooner? Her mother kept a list of club members for Aunt Em. She clicked it open and ran her eyes down the names: Anna Klimas, Dalia Stone. If Everett was a member, by her mother's alphabetization method, his name should have been next, but it wasn't there.

The bathroom door opened and Helma jumped, then quietly closed the file and shut the computer before folding her hands together on the table top.

"Will you make us hot water for tea, Wilhelmina?" Aunt Em asked.

While Helma found cups and saucers and boiled water, Aunt Em sat at the table and pondered the recovered *Stelmužė* box.

Helma heard her murmuring and glimpsed her turning it in her hands, nodding. Then the teapot shrieked and a stream of water burst from the spout and Helma leapt into action to clean it up.

When she finally carried the tea to the table on a tray, Aunt Em's joy in the return of the *Stelmužė* box had disappeared. Her face was wet, her shoulders bowed as if in grief. "What's wrong, Aunt Em?"

Aunt Em swayed in her chair and tapped the carved box, but was unable to speak.

"Is something wrong with the box?" Helma asked, resting a hand on Aunt Em's thin shoulder to steady her.

"No, the box is fine. It's only sad."

"There are sad memories in it?" Helma asked.

Aunt Em shook her head. "No. Nothing is inside."

CHAPTER 16

A Cat of a Different Stripe

"And then," Helma told Ruth, "she wouldn't say another word about her *Stelmužė* box or the robbery, or the 999."

They sat in Saul's Deli, Ruth eating what she called a "snack," a chocolate-mint milkshake and an order of onion rings drenched in catsup. Helma sipped at a cup of peppermint tea.

"Hmm," Ruth said while she shook a layer of salt across her catsup until it sparkled like new snow. "Beloved aunt and mother are robbed by two men. Forget for a minute that one robber plummeted to his death through the window, conveniently splattering himself across the parking lot." She raised a catsup-covered onion ring to Helma, "Gruesome. Sorry," and continued around a mouthful. "So the living robber returns stolen items without a word of explanation. What does that tell you?"

"It tells me he regrets his crime," Helma said. "At least the robbery. We still don't know how or why the other robber went out the window."

"I think he's trying to worm his way into your good graces."

"How could he be trying to impress me if he's returning the items anonymously?" Helma asked reasonably." I have no idea who's responsible."

"Ah, the mysterious criminal mind." She waved across Saul's at a tall man who nodded and quickly looked away. "Who knows; maybe he's thinking it'll look good during his murder trial. What did the groom-to-be say about Em's returned box?"

Helma was silent and Ruth turned her attention to shaking the last of her milkshake from the metal cup into her empty fluted glass. "You didn't tell him?"

"I intend to."

"But you wanted my opinion first. I'm flattered."

"I thought if we discussed the crime aloud, I could make more sense of it before I talked to Wayne." She paused to ask the waitress for more hot water for her tea.

"Where were the packages mailed from?" Ruth asked.

"Aunt Em's *Stelmužė* box was mailed in Bellehaven, but the stamp on the envelope that held my mother's wedding ring wasn't canceled."

Ruth nodded sagely. "I get letters like that sometimes. If you're really careful you can peel off the stamp and reuse it."

"But for the ring to have arrived so soon after the crime, it's more probable it was slipped into my mailbox, in person."

"That's creepy. So the criminal's local, and he's got his eye on you. Geesh, Helma, stick close to your intended."

"It could still be someone who took the items off the dead robber before the police arrived and is suffering guilt. He or she saw the robber fall. Or the items flew out of his hands as he... landed, and he or she picked them up."

"Ya' know, your Aunt Em, as much as I love her, just might be delusional about there being a second robber."

"At first, when the incident was fresh in her mind, she did believe there was only a single robber," Helma conceded.

"Yeah. All this searching for a second criminal might be a hopeless fantasy. There was only one robber who for some mysterious reason went out your aunt's window. Enter our good citizen with a guilty conscience who's returning items he picked up near the body. End of story."

"And who also recognized me," Helma added.

"That's what comes from being in the public eye. The library's a stage and you have a very large audience."

The man Ruth had waved to walked past their table carrying a plastic basket containing a sandwich and coleslaw. He paused, took a deep breath and said to Ruth in a rush of words, "Looking for a man who's perfect is a good way to remain single." And he walked away without another word.

Ruth looked after him, made a motion across her chest as if she were writing on it, and said, "Well, that was a T-shirt moment."

Helma glanced at her watch. Ruth followed her glance. "You're keeping your appointment with Mr. Dubois?" She drawled out his name.

"This is the last one. The wedding is a year away, at least. It's too soon."

"Just admit it: you don't want his help."

"I don't want his help."

Ruth guffawed. "What about the pink shoebox? Did you find out what that was about?"

"It was a bottle of Lithuanian liquor, from Lithuania, called 999."

"Really?" Ruth's interest brightened considerably. "Smuggled?"

"Of course not. But it's only available in Lithuania so it had to be purchased by someone visiting the country."

"Our little friend from Joker's?" Ruth guessed.

"Aunt Em won't tell me."

"No reason not to, unless he was only the delivery boy and she's covering for somebody else."

"I'm going to ask Dalia Stone at the Lithuanian club," Helma told her.

"Hah. Smuggled. Like in the olden days. Em must feel like she's back in business."

"I beg your pardon?"

"C'mon, Helm. During Prohibition half the population in the county where we spent our tender years was distilling liquid goodies for Chicago, everybody knew those stories. And half of our beloved county was Lithuanian. So...there you go."

"That was an unfounded rumor, and — "

"I know: you don't listen to rumors." Ruth smugly loaded the last of her catsup on the last onion ring. "Just because you don't believe it doesn't mean it isn't true."

Mr. Dubois had left his door ajar. Soft piano music and the fragrance of flowers drifted from his apartment to Helma. She was about to knock when he opened it wide as if he'd been standing behind the gap.

"Come in, my dear," he said, bowing slightly and waving her inside. He wore the same clothes he'd worn on their first meeting, and now she saw that although his linen pants were sharply creased, the pant leg hems had a "nubby" look, as if they'd been dry-cleaned too many times.

Two delicate tea cups and a matching porcelain teapot sat on the table, and arranged beside those were swatches of pale-hued shiny fabric, photos of bridal dresses, and sheets of paper bearing samples of elaborate print fonts.

Exhaustion swept over Helma, exhaustion so deep she had to briefly close her eyes, causing Mr. Dubois to inquire, "Are you all right, Wilhelmina? Such a lovely name: Wilhelmina. Regal. Come sit down. I'll pour you a cup of tea."

"I think better standing," Helma said, not moving.

"What can I do? What will give you comfort?" His eyes grew large in concern. His hands hovered over her without touching.

"Mr. Dubois," she began. "I'm not of the blushing bride persuasion..."

"We can design around a sophisticated theme." Again that indefinable accent: not French, not Spanish. "Black is very popular this season. You'd be lovely in black."

"In black I'd resemble a remaindered Halloween figure. No, I prefer a more simple—"

"We can be simple," he enthused. "Pearls, an ivory suit, the groom in soft gray, your makeup understated."

"—something simple that I choose myself," Helma finished. "I realize my mother and aunt meant well, but you see, my wedding is a long way off, at least a year, and I'm still accustoming myself to the idea," Helma said in rare personal disclosure. "I'm not ready to begin planning."

Mr. Dubois studied her a few moments before he spoke. "A year is too far away, my dear," he said gently.

"At least a year. My mother and aunt are over-enthusiastic."

His hand hovered near her elbow. "Come sit down. Let's talk." His accent disappeared; his voice grew subdued, without artifice. "I think you're onto me," he said, smiling at her.

Helma did as he beckoned, sitting in a white chair in his white living room while he poured tea into both cups, nudging one cup toward her before he sat down.

"I'm long retired," he said and raised his cup to his lips, but Helma could tell he hadn't actually sipped any liquid. "I haven't really worked in the movie or fashion world in decades. And what I did then was minor. No big movie stars, no memorable names." He nodded to the signed photo of himself with the beautiful woman. "She was probably my biggest star. Do you know who she is?"

"I'm sorry, but I don't," Helma admitted.

"Neither does anybody else." He laughed briefly. "I've created a bit of mystique around myself, but in reality..."

"If you need...clients," Helma said delicately, "I may know of someone who would be interested."

He laughed again, but kindly. "Thank you, my dear, but I'm quite comfortably out of the business. I only came out of retirement because of your aunt."

"She can be persuasive."

He smoothed back his yellow hair. "I'm sure she can be. She is a remarkable woman, as I've discovered during our many long conversations. Remarkable bone structure, and those eyes..." He shook his head, his own eyes distant. "When she was young – "

"You knew Aunt Em when she was young?"

He blinked. "Of course not, but a man in my business can see what underlies skin in all its permutations." He paused. "And what lies behind the eyes, too."

Helma recognized when someone was being evasive. "Are you saying Aunt Em confides in you?"

"Perhaps a little."

"Did she confide in you regarding her robbery? Or her stolen carved box, her *Stelmužė* box?"

"Those are transitory things," he said dismissively. He gazed at Helma. "She's convinced her time is growing short, you know. I've learned to respect that awareness in a contemporary. They're usually right."

Helma was silent, digesting what he'd just said. She didn't feel the shock she'd expect those words to cause. Hadn't that fear been lurking just outside her own consciousness? Aunt Em's vagueness, her plan to move to the second floor. "She's *told* you that?" Helma asked, still not ready to accept his assessment.

"Not in those exact words," he admitted, and Helma couldn't help exhaling in relief. He could very well be wrong, doing what she'd heard a psychologist she'd been unfortunately coerced into listening to, call, "projecting his own fears" on Aunt Em. He was old himself, older than he appeared.

"But she did express hope that you'd move up your wedding date." He smiled. "I suspect she hoped I'd persuade you by mentioning *your* mature years though, not hers."

Helma set her untouched tea on the coffee table and rose. "Thank you, Mr. Dubois. I'm very grateful for your honesty."

"So you're declining my skilled assistance for your wedding?" he asked lightly. Beneath his smile, Helma saw the touch of hurt.

"In the way Aunt Em originally intended," Helma told him. "But I'd be appreciative if, when I do make plans, you'd look over them and give me suggestions."

"I'd be honored."

Helma's mother answered the door, waved Helma inside, and hurried back to the dining room table. "Just let me close this file," she said, as she worked a few keys and closed the computer lid, asking distractedly, "How was your appointment with Mr. Dubois?"

"He was very helpful. Where's Aunt Em?"

"In bed already, sound asleep. Now, about this morning, Helma. TNT and I have known each other a very long time..."

"It's fine, Mother, really. I think you and TNT will be happy together."

"You do?"

"I do. What were you working on on your computer?"

"My new file. Lists of what to take to TNT's apartment, which items to sell, which things we won't need. What do you think of that hunk of machinery he has in his living room?" She made up-and-down arm-flexing movements.

"His weight machine? He works out on it every day. I hear him sometimes through the walls. I believe it's very important to him."

"I wonder..."

She felt a momentary pang for TNT. "When will you begin moving?"

"When Em's settled. Not before."

"Did she tell you about the return of her *Stelmužė* box?"

"Yes. Isn't that interesting?"

Interesting? Lillian was distracted, distracted from the robbery and the dead man, distracted from Helma's wedding, from Aunt Em's move to the second floor. Her focus had totally shifted to TNT.

The power of love.

"Mother," Helma said, waiting until her mother looked at her, although she wasn't sure how dedicated her mother's attention really was. "If Grandpa carved the box and gave it to Aunt Em, did he give similar boxes to all of his children?"

"Oh, Helma. How would I know? There were six of them, remember? And they weren't exactly the most responsible group." She made flapping motions with her hands. "You could never count on them for anything except to raise hell. I remember that time -"

"Did he carve a box for Dad?" she asked.

Her brow wrinkled. "If he did, I never saw it. It wasn't among his things after he died, and I looked through everything. If I'd snooped sooner, I might have found out—"

"He was the youngest," Helma said, avoiding another well-worn tale.

"And she's the oldest," Lillian said. "So maybe he only carved one for her, one of those passing-down things, like her amber necklace, which we all know goes to you, despite what your cousin Ricky thinks, but it would have gone to her oldest daughter if she'd thought to have children."

"I see." Helma stifled a yawn. "Aunt Em told me about the 999."

Lillian rolled her eyes. "She acted like she'd been handed gold the way she tucked it away, or maybe she was trying to hide it from the police, I don't know. Smuggling at her age."

"It's not illegal to bring 999 into the country," she reminded her mother.

"Maybe not, but it's a crime what she paid that boy for it."

"Who was he?" Helma asked, "Do you know his name?"

"Not his last name, but his first is Barber or Blake, maybe Bill, something that starts with a B." Lillian clicked her mouse and frowned at the screen. "That little transaction was all Em's doing. I had absolutely nothing to do with it."

"Does she have a friend in the Lithuanian club named Everett?"

"I don't know. Ask her next time you see her." She looked up at Helma. "You're not asking if she has a *romantic* friend, are you?"

"No," Helma said, and then amended, "I don't think so. Has she mentioned the carving knife the police found on the floor?" She couldn't help it: she glanced at the unmarred carpet where the police had gathered around the knife.

"No," Lillian said emphatically, "and don't you remind her of it." She shuddered. "It would give her nightmares. When I think of what... Well, just don't even say one word about it."

As Helma opened the door to leave, her mother called, "Throw a kiss to TNT when you pass his apartment." She closed the door on her mother's low laughter.

"I've been trying to catch you all day, so finally I decided to just come over and make sure everything was all right."

"It's been a very busy day," Helma told Wayne. "Come in." She opened the door all the way for him and he stepped inside, taking her in his arms before she had time to think. Helma had a highly developed sense of the transit of seconds, minutes, and hours, and it was always a shock how personal closeness to Wayne Gallant skewed her sense of time's flight. So much so that when his arms relaxed she checked the clock over her stove to reorient herself.

"I had an interesting conversation with your manager," Wayne said.

"Walter David?"

He nodded, a quizzical look on his face. "He seemed to think your cat is a bad influence on his cat. Boy Cat Zukas is neutered, right?"

"He is. I found Moggy on my balcony, wet and dirty."

"And Boy Cat Zukas was with her?"

"On the railing. He and Moggy had a relationship once, but certainly they wouldn't remember it."

Wayne grinned and glanced over at Boy Cat Zukas who lay curled in his basket with one eye open in that disturbing manner he had. "Never underestimate a cat."

"Do you like cats?" she asked.

"Some cats."

"He was a stray cat, originally, and I never intended to adopt him. It was a matter of urgency at the time. He's probably used to being a stray and may not care where he lives. He kills things. And he's stubborn and disobedient and..."

Wayne touched Helma's cheek. "We'll put up with him. When I bought my house, there was a cat entrance in the back door. It'll be a cinch to unblock it." He paused. "I'm being presumptuous, assuming you want to live in my house, that is." That pause again, the expression on his face that was usually accompanied by the jangle of keys in his pocket, or the silent tapping of his foot. "Do you? I mean, will you? You and..." He nodded toward Boy Cat Zukas.

"I do, I mean, we, will. We, that is, I, would like to," Helma told him, for some reason needing to catch her breath. "He'll come, too."

Wayne's house was situated on a bluff at the north end of town, with a long view of Washington Bay and the Olympic Peninsula beyond. "My mother's moving in with TNT, next door to my apartment," she added, and then felt her cheeks pinken as she realized she'd made that totally unrelated fact connote a reason to move into Wayne's house.

He laughed. "That'll make four happy people, then."

"Four? Oh. Us, too."

Their talk moved to the crime, and Wayne reached inside his pocket and pulled out the plastic evidence bag containing her mother's ring. "We're finished with this: no evidence on it. Either you can return it to your mother..." he swallowed, "or I will."

"I'll give it to her," Helma offered, and he set the plastic bag on her coffee table, relief visible in his every movement. "But that reminds me," she began, thinking it would have been preferable to have told him this over the telephone where she could escape his sharp policeman's eyes.

His face grew alert. "Yes?"

"I received Aunt Em's *Stelmužė* box in an anonymous package at the library today."

"Was it mailed or delivered to you?"

"Mailed—from the Bellehaven post office, but no return address, no explanation."

"Where is it?" he asked, glancing around her apartment.

"I gave it to her."

"And you told Carter?"

"No, I didn't. It seemed more imperative to restore the box to Aunt Em. She's been very upset."

"And was she satisfied?" he asked, as if he detected hesitation in Helma's voice, which she was positive wasn't there.

"Not really. I think it's all been a trial: the robbery and death, all the memories of her family. She's the oldest sibling in a large family and the last one alive, so the box reminded her of all she's lost."

Helma considered asking his help to discover who'd supplied Aunt Em with the 999, then decided no, not while there was even the slightest chance Aunt Em was teetering on the brink of illegal activity.

"Did she reveal what was inside the box?" Wayne asked.

"It's only a decorative carving. She said there was nothing inside it."

He raised his right eyebrow. "Nothing was ever inside the box—or nothing is inside it now?"

Helma tried to recall Aunt Em's exact words and her expression as she'd spoken. "She was relieved to have it returned," she told Wayne, carefully remembering. "And then later she became emotional. But the box, if that's what it is, doesn't have a clasp or any way to open it. I even shook it and nothing shifted inside."

"A secret mechanism?"

"I don't see how. It's a very small box."

"We have tools to let us see inside solid-looking objects," he said, and Helma heard the faintest trace of reproach in his voice. "Can you ask your aunt to let me take a look at it?"

"I doubt if she'll let it out of her sight again."

He was silent, and Helma asked, "You wouldn't subpoena it from her, would you?"

"It may not have much relevance to the case, but that makes two stolen items that were returned to you." He motioned toward her mother's ring. "And we don't know why. Tell me more about this box...Stil- ?"

"*Stelmužė*. It's a village in northern Lithuania and the site of a famous ancient tree. Supposedly the wood is from the tree. Of course, there's no way to know that."

"There is, but it sounds like a story that's better left a mystery."

Helma nodded, imagining Aunt Em's crushing disappointment if the oak wood wasn't connected to Stelmužė after all. "It's very intricately carved, every square inch. Aunt Em may not let you take it, but I'm sure she'd let you examine it."

"Good. Let's do that."

"Do you have more information on the deceased robber?"

"Chip Block." He sighed. "We're still looking for a connection," and Helma knew there was no new evidence.

CHAPTER 17

To Catch a Smuggler

After Wayne left, Helma checked her Bellehaven phone book and ran her finger down the list of Stones. When she reached J and D Stone she jotted the number on the note pad beside her telephone before she dialed it. A man answered. "She's at the club," he responded curtly.

"The Lithuanian Club?" Helma asked.

"I guess."

Her watch read a few minutes before nine o'clock. "When do you expect her home?"

"Beats me. She gets all wrapped up in that place. Don't call her after nine-thirty, okay?"

"Thank you," Helma told him, and hung up. She was still dressed, and the Lithuanian Club was only across town, not that far in a small city like Bellehaven. She quickly combed her hair and smoothed her lips with pink lipstick.

Helma let Ruth's phone ring ten times—a sign Ruth had turned off her answering machine—hung up just as the eleventh ring began, and immediately dialed Ruth's number again. This time it rang five times.

"What?" Ruth demanded, sounding ready to repulse an assault, and Helma nearly broke the connection.

"I'm dropping by the Lithuanian Club to ask Dalia Stone a few questions. Would you like to come with me?"

"Isn't it a little late for 'dropping by'? What do you need, back-up or protection?"

"You often have good ideas in new situations."

"For protection, you mean," Ruth said glumly. "Sure. It's better than the big fat zero that's happening here. I'll be in my driveway waiting. What weapons should I bring?"

"No weapons, Ruth."

"That's what you say."

Ruth sat on the big rock that edged into the alley, dressed totally in black. Helma would have missed her if Ruth hadn't been wearing boots with silver reflecting strips on the heels.

"So the Lithuanians did it?" Ruth asked as she climbed inside. Helma swept her eyes over Ruth's short leather jacket and black pants; she didn't *see* a weapon. "There has to be a good reason for rushing off to the Lithuanian club in the middle of the night."

"By definition," Helma explained, "'middle of the night' is the time period equidistant between the hours darkness begins and ends, which at this time of year is approximately one a.m.. And it's only 9:18."

"It's dark and that makes it the middle of the night," Ruth said, fastening her seat belt with exaggerated motions. "What's up?"

"Aunt Em won't divulge who procured the 999 for her, so I plan to ask Dalia Stone about the blond man. He may belong to the Lithuanian club." Her Buick's headlights caught the glare of two round eyes near a garbage can. They flashed and disappeared.

"So you plan to hold her feet to the fire? What? You think she'll confess the club's a front for a giant smuggling ring?"

"I don't believe that. But there are some curious coincidences."

"And the coincidences all begin with the letter L." Ruth ticked off on her fingers. "Two ladies with Lithuanian genes robbed, stolen Lithuanian box, returned Lithuanian box, smuggled Lithuanian booze. I detect a theme."

"Possibly," Helma said as they turned onto Holby Street. Few cars traveled the streets of Bellehaven as if it really *were* the middle of the night.

Have you ever tasted the stuff, this 999?"

"Of course, but not for years. It's very potent."

"I thought you said you couldn't import 999, so where'd you drink it?"

"999 is the commercial version, but it's based on an old—possibly ancient—recipe. A likeness can be brewed, with the proper herbs and grain alcohol." She remembered again the tattered, handwritten recipe that she'd seen at Aunt Em's. "It's very volatile."

"My kind of drink. Would she let me have a taste? Expand my alcoholic knowledge?"

"I'm sure she would."

The front door of the Lithuanian Club was unlocked, and as Helma and Ruth entered, Dalia Stone glanced up from the dust mop she was pushing the length of the meeting room. A tall man with his back to them stacked folded chairs with unnecessary vigor and sound

"Hello, again," Dalia called cheerily when she saw Ruth and Helma in the entry. "You're too late for our meeting."

"I'd like to ask you a couple of questions if you have a moment," Helma told her.

"Certainly. Can you finish this, Bronus?"

The young man stepped closer to take the dust mop and Helma wasn't terribly surprised to find herself facing the young man she'd spied giving Aunt Em the pink shoebox. The same young man she'd seen in the library and who she'd tried to question at Joker's bar.

"It's Bruno, Mom," he grumbled.

"But it's Bronus in Lithuanian."

"That's three generations ago," he protested. "This is now."

Dalia held out the mop to him. "And it's *your* heritage."

In that curious way of the young to not quite "see" those older than themselves, his eyes at first passed unawares over Helma and Ruth, until Ruth growled, "Hey, *you*," and then recognition snapped his eyes into focus, followed rapidly by embarrassment, guilt, wariness, and finally defiance winning out.

In the well-lit room he definitely didn't appear old enough to purchase alcohol. His slouch emphasized the wide shoulders that hadn't yet filled out.

"You shaved off the..." Ruth said, motioning toward his face. Helma would have found it difficult to describe that wisp of hair as a beard, too.

Bruno cast a dark look at his mother, who raised her chin and said. "If a child lives under *my* roof, he has to follow *my* rules."

"Child?" Ruth squeaked out. "You still live at home?" She raised her hand to her forehead as if she were about to begin a vigorous massage. "How old are you, anyway? Like *exactly* how old?"

It was Dalia who answered. "He's twenty-two," and Ruth relaxed. "He was dismissed from college," Dalia went on. "Through his own fault. No job. No place to live."

"I make money." Bruno leaned the dust mop against the wall and jammed his hands in his jeans pockets.

"That's not the same as a *job*, where you show up for specific hours and a real employer writes you a regular paycheck." Dalia sounded as if it were a recurring conversation. She reclaimed the dust mop and held it toward Bruno, who didn't reach for it.

"My aunt recently purchased a bottle of 999 from you," Helma said.

"Bruno!" Dalia cried. She released the dust mop and it clattered to the floor.

Bruno gave a dramatic sigh and picked up the mop. "Yeah?"

"Another bottle. Just how many did you bring back?"

"Mom..."

"We sent him to visit relatives near Vilnius," she told Helma and Ruth. "For two weeks, and when he comes home the next thing we know he's bought himself a new computer. No job, but he's treating his friends to movies. He turned himself into a one-man tourist shop with all the 'merchandise' he brought back. The worst was the 999. All three kinds."

Bruno sulked, Dalia was red-faced, Helma was curious, and Ruth nodded, saying, "Clever kid."

"He charged people five times what he paid for it," Dalia said, and when Bruno looked down at the floor, she added, "At least five times. How much money did your aunt give him?"

"I don't know," Helma told her. "She wouldn't tell me."

"You march right over there and give her back every single penny," Dalia scolded Bruno as if he were twelve, not twenty-two.

"If I might intervene," Helma ventured. "My aunt understood what she was paying for and she's very happy to have the 999. If Bruno returned her money, she'd feel duty-bound to return the 999, which would be a loss for her. I'd really prefer she kept the liquor."

"That'll be another two months of helping me here, then," Dalia told Bruno, who trudged back to the furthest corner of the meeting room, dragging the dust mop behind him, dismissed.

"Don't play the game if you don't want the shame, kid," Ruth said to his back.

Dalia scowled at Ruth and said to Helma, "I'm really sorry your aunt was caught up in his little smuggling business. He'll end up joining the mafia, I swear."

"Will he be visiting Lithuania again soon?" Helma asked.

"If he does, he'll have to save up his own money to get there."

"Do you know anyone planning a trip to Lithuania in the near future?"

"Not in the club. The Kubildises are planning a trip in November. Is there something you'd like from the Baltics?"

"No. I was just curious. My aunt has a beautiful carved wooden box her father made for her. Are you familiar with similar boxes?"

Helma made the shape of a small rectangle with her hands, at the same time keeping an eye on Bruno. His face was plainly visible. If he were paying attention, and certainly she was speaking loud enough it wouldn't take any effort on his part, the mention of Aunt Em's box didn't spark any response from him.

"I've seen some beautiful carving. Geometric or folk figures?"

"Geometric. It appears to be a box, but it may just be a carved block of oak."

"Ask one of the old... original Lithuanians in the club about it. Anna Klimas collects wood carvings, mostly figures, but she might be able to tell you. We're having a luncheon tomorrow for Rimas's family before they leave the area. Bring your aunt."

"Thank you. If she's able, we'll be here." Helma paused. "Do you come to the library often?"

"Sometimes. Why?" Dalia frowned toward Bruno who was swishing his mop back and forth, banging it against the floor trim.

"I first met your son when he accompanied a man called Everett to the library. Do you know him?"

"Sure. He's one of the original Lithuanians from before World War II. Bruno runs errands for him since his daughter called the police and had his driver's license taken away. Come tomorrow and you'll meet him."

"Stop and say hello the next time you visit the library," Helma invited her. "We recently purchased two highly-praised books on living with adult children. I'll set them aside for you."

"Listen, can you swing by Books & Nicknacks?"

"If you need to buy a book, Ruth, we can stop at Village Books. It's closer, and it's open until ten tonight." Helma would have suggested the library as an alternative to the chain bookstore, but Ruth still owed over eighty dollars in library fines and was banned from borrowing library materials until she paid up. Despite what Helma might call Ruth's "badgering," she refused to borrow books for Ruth.

"No. I have to pick up something from a clerk who works there. It'll just take a sec."

Books & Nicknacks was only a block off their route, so Helma obliged, turning into the paved lot and parking her Buick in a row that held two hybrid cars and a yellow motor scooter.

"There are plenty of spaces back there," Ruth grumbled, looking over her shoulder at the store's entrance across the parking lot.

"It's beneficial to add exercise to our daily routine wherever possible," Helma explained.

"Then you could have warned me to bring my hiking boots. Come on."

"You said your errand would only take a second."

"Well, sure, but I have to find him first."

Books & Nooknacks smelled of coffee and chocolate, and reminded Helma of Hugie's grocery store with its deep greens and dark woods and colorful displays. Only instead of cleverly arranged soup cans and oranges: books.

As with any confirmed librarian, Helma was helpless in the presence of thousands of books, succumbing to a burgeoning sense of good will, a certain, well…itch, in the fingers to stroke new covers and sniff high-rag-content paper, to flip to the back of nonfiction titles to study the depth of indexes, her eyes registering of their own volition the alphabetical accuracy of authors' placement within subject areas.

"Amuse yourself," Ruth said. "I'll be right back."

Helma pulled her attention away from the books to see Ruth striding toward a young man ducking behind a rack of financial planning books. Apropos, Ruth was calling in her big voice, "Hey, Jack. You know that twenty I loaned you? It wasn't a gift."

A loose child ran past Helma, dropping a picture book. She picked it up and returned it to the children's department, then she recommended one tree identification book over another to a young woman dressed in sweats similar to TNT's, and directed another woman to the restrooms.

She paused near a prominent display of bestsellers, drawn by its familiarity.

Fanned and artfully stacked, the books mirrored the titles on Ms. Moon's display in the library. Helma tucked an uneven title back into alignment and noted the publisher, then noted the publisher on another arrangement of three books.

Curious, she circled the display, reading titles and publishers. Against an instrumental version of a David Bowie song, Ruth's voice rose in the distance, the phrase, "I'd prefer it sooner, like now," detectable amid a hot stream of words.

"May I help you?" a cheerful man in a green plaid kilt asked Helma.

"Yes. May I speak to whoever's in charge of product placement?" she asked, smiling.

"I'm Em's niece," Helma told Rimas Klimas's sister Anna on the telephone. "May I come visit you for a few minutes?"

"Did Emily die?" Anna asked.

"Oh no," Helma told her, gasping at the thought. "I have a Lithuanian question for you."

"Ask me now."

"It's easier for me to speak in person," Helma told her. Also easier to surmise when someone was lying.

Anna Klimas sighed and gave Helma her address. She lived in Treasure Oaks, assisted living apartments at the edge of Bellehaven, among tidy buildings with large parking lots and quiet, litter-free grounds—an area often referred to in the *Bellehaven Daily News* as "clean industry."

"I'm not one of those old ladies losing my brain that I need to be here," she told Helma sternly as if Helma had challenged her. "I just have slow hands and legs."

"I'll be there in fifteen minutes."

"Wait," Anna said. "Did you say you worked at the library?"

Helma hadn't, but Aunt Em may have told her. "I'm a librarian at the Bellehaven Public Library," Helma admitted.

"Can you bring me that new Carolyn Hart book, then?"

Treasure Oaks consisted of a single story, built in the shape of an H, with a dining room and exercise facilities in the center. It was simple, light, clean, and far more sedate than the Silver Gables. A woman holding a tray of juice and Mars bars directed Helma to Anna Klimas's apartment. "Her name's on the door," she told Helma. "Want one?" She offered her tray of juice and candy.

"No thank you."

"Anna K." read a sign decorated with cowboys beside an ajar door. Helma tapped lightly. There was no answer.

"You've gotta knock louder than that around here if you want to be heard," a man pushing a walker past warned her. "Anna's a little..." He tapped his ear.

She did, bruising her knuckles, and was rewarded by a voice calling, "Come in."

Helma recognized the woman sitting in the recliner from the photo at the Lithuanian Club of the woman gazing down at Rimas's body. She sat on an island, surrounded by TV trays and coffee tables: a heavy woman with short, white hair in a new permanent of tight curls, and wearing the same style of dress as Aunt Em had begun donning: loose prints with zippers or snaps up the front. She appeared to be in her eighties.

"I'm Helma Zukas," she introduced herself, and set the Carolyn Hart book on a coffee table far enough from a cup of tea to protect it from any sloshing.

Anna nodded. "You look like Em."

"Thank you," Helma told her, and the woman snorted. "Dalia Stone suggested you might be able to help me."

"You wanted to speak of Lithuania?" She paused and narrowed her eyes. "Or Emily's crime?"

Helma moved a straight-back chair from the dinette to Anna's living room and sat facing her. "One of the items my aunt lost in the robbery was a small oak box, heavily carved. I thought you might be able to tell me more about it."

She frowned. "Can't Em?" she asked, and then she nodded to herself. A slight smile flicked across her lips. "Ah, her memory. Such a shame. I'm older than she is and I don't forget so much."

Anna gestured toward a small bookcase, one shelf filled with a variety of wood carvings, many that Helma recognized: the sorrowful man, women with braids as thick as their arms, figures with inhumanly huge hands and feet, ogres and odd bearded figures. "These are my wood carvings. I have more in boxes in my closet. I change them on the first day of every month, like in a museum."

She admired the carvings, picking up the sorrowful man and noting the fine details. "Have you been collecting the carvings very long?"

"I had a few, but when people are stuck to buy me a present, they buy me a carving. From here to there," she said, sweeping her hand to demonstrate either time, or a burgeoning collection of wood carvings; Helma wasn't sure.

"Aunt Em's box was carved with Lithuanian geometric designs, like weaving."

"I remember it from when I visited with your aunt once."

"You saw it?" Helma asked, shaping her hands to illustrate the small rectangle, just as she had for Dalia.

Anna nodded and lifted a glass of pink liquid. "And you're wondering if I stole it?"

"No. I'm wondering about its significance. Her father carved it for her."

Anna shrugged. "It's personal, then, a...memento."

"It doesn't seem to open. Do you recall such boxes as a girl?"

"Perhaps." The woman sipped the pick liquid, then dabbed a tissue against her upper lip. "Ah, secrets. We love our secrets. Maybe there was something special about the design."

"Aunt Em said the wood is from an oak tree in Stelmužė."

She raised her eyebrows. "Now that *is* special. The tree in Stelmužė is too old to count, over a thousand years. I have a picture somewhere..." She looked around her apartment, then shrugged.

"A fence is around the tree now so no one can take its wood. People steal every acorn to plant, but they won't grow - nowhere but in Lithuania." Anna nodded sagely. "A piece of that tree is precious. It doesn't have to be a box—just a block of the wood is good enough."

"I saw the photos of your brother's funeral. All of your family together."

Anna set her glass on a tray. "Next time we all get together will be when I die."

"You said you'd given him a proper Lithuanian send off?"

"We sang the *Angelus* and kept watch. Dunate brought herbs. We all kissed him farewell." She smiled. "And then we drank too much whiskey. He will rest in peace. Bring Em tomorrow for the lunch and she can meet my family." Her old eyes squinted. "My family is good for bragging about, too, not just hers."

"I'll ask her, thank you," Helma said, and left, thinking as she walked to her car that Anna Klimas was the type of woman who never gave all she had or told all she knew, that she always held something back, just in case.

CHAPTER 18

The Positive Side of Pot Lucks

"I'm coming with you. I have a bone to pick with your aunt," Ruth said, leaning over the wall of Helma's cubicle. Her eyes sparked dangerously, but Helma felt a curious sense of relief. Sparks were preferable to Ruth's dull-eyed depression.

"Are you painting again?" she asked Ruth.

"What's that got to do with anything? She is one underhanded lady."

"What did she do?"

"She..." Ruth stopped. "Well, actually, seeing how she's one of our frail elderly, I have to make her confess before I shake her reasons out of her."

"Ruth, I will not allow you to bully Aunt Em. You can tell me and I will discreetly discuss your issue with her. But you can't confront her."

"I won't talk about it with anybody but her." Ruth blew out her lower lip. "Okay, so what if I very nicely hint around a little? She balks and I clam up, okay?"

Helma cautiously agreed; she was confident she could protect Aunt Em from being badgered, and taking her to the luncheon would definitely be easier if there were two of them. Her mother had declined, stating airily she had to "go shopping" with TNT.

Planning for Helma and Wayne's marriage had been swept away by Lillian's scheme to create an "all new" home with

TNT, which would include none of their previous belongings. "Everything untouched by anyone else," Lillian had rhapsodized.

While Aunt Em was involved in what she termed as "powdering up," Helma gave her mother the recovered wedding ring.

"I didn't expect to ever see it again." Lillian gazed down at the irregular gold circle, thinned and scratched, in her palm. "The silly old thing. A pawn shop won't give me five dollars for it."

"Mother, you're not planning to *sell* it, are you?"

She closed her fingers into a fist around the ring. "I should, just because he made me so mad. If he'd—" She stopped, looking deeply into Helma's eyes. "Oh dear, I don't really mean that. Your father – he really was a good man. He was just so...*much*."

"Where are we going again?" Aunt Em asked after Helma and Ruth had settled her in the front seat and Helma had pulled away from the Silver Gables.

"To the Lithuanian Club. It's a luncheon for Rimas's family."

Aunt Em smoothed the lap of her black dress and nodded. "He died, didn't he? And I missed the funeral."

"That's right, but they understood. And his sister Anna will be very happy you're coming to the lunch."

"Anna," she said, half-closing her gnarled hands and butting them together like fists.

"I thought you were friends."

"Sometimes. Sometimes not."

"I want to ask you why—" Ruth began, but when Helma turned and gave her a warning glance, she finished, "Keep your eyes on the road, Helma. You're driving like a loose wheel."

"What did you say, Ruthie?" Aunt Em asked.

"Nothing. I'll tell you over lunch."

There were about twenty-five people at the luncheon, most of them Rimas's family, and the majority of those would be returning to Chicago, Massachusetts, or Pennsylvania in the next twenty-four hours. Paper-covered folding tables had been set up in the meeting room and lunch had already begun, even though Helma, Ruth, and Aunt Em were exactly on time.

"I'm so happy you could make it," Dalia Stone said, hugging Aunt Em. Behind her, her son Bruno sullenly hung up coats, his face averted from the activity.

Old cookbooks had been unearthed. *Kugelis*, *zeppelinas*, *šaltebaršai*, bacon buns, even pickled herring, and one red gelatin salad with miniature marshmallows and mandarin oranges stirred into it.

Ruth's plate was laden to heaping. She dug into it with a fork in one hand and knife in the other, pausing every little while to say "Mm-mm-mmm." Helma's plate held three slices of *kugelis* spread with sour cream, and two bacon buns. She'd skip dinner to make up for it.

Anna Klimas lowered herself into a chair across the table from Aunt Em, the two women's conversation painfully polite.

"Your robbery is solved?" Anna asked Aunt Em.

"Almost," Aunt Em told her. "Helma and the chief are wrapping it up. He will be her husband, you know."

"I heard that. Your niece asked me about that box of yours that was stolen."

Aunt Em frowned at Helma, then inquired sweetly of Anna, "She thought *you* took it?"

"No, but I am an expert on carving." Anna raised her chin. "She needed my advice."

Aunt Em shook her head at Helma as if she'd committed a gauche act.

And at that moment, as if a memory had flashed through her mind, Aunt Em jerked her head and gaped at Anna, her eyes widening.

"Are you all right, Aunt Em?" Helma asked.

"I almost remembered something." She touched her fore-head, and added with a sheepish expression, "but now it's gone."

"This is my nephew, John," Anna told Aunt Em, reaching to touch the sleeve of a middle-aged man and tug him closer. "He is an accountant. Very big firm. Tell her some of your clients, John."

John, the nephew, was a big man, in all directions. He looked pained, then patted his aunt's shoulder and said breezily, "Can't do it, Aunt Anna, I'd be telling secrets." And he winked at Aunt Em.

"See?" Anna whispered to Aunt Em. "Big names. And that's my great niece Pamela with her little boy, isn't he darling?" She gazed around the small group, chattering and eating.

"My nephew Tony came all the way from Chicago to Rimas's funeral. You met him once, remember? The head of the Traffic Department said he couldn't run Chicago without Tony. And him so young, too."

"It is sad people have to die so you are able to see your relatives," Aunt Em said, and Ruth snorted on a soup spoon of bright pink *šaltebaršai*.

Anna shook her gray head as if she'd sniffed a rude order, and pulled herself up to standing with the aid of her walker.

"*Viso gero*," Aunt Em said pleasantly. Goodbye.

"Now, Em," Ruth said when her soup bowl was empty, "why did you send Detective Carter Houston to my house?"

Aunt Em's eyes widened. "I don't remember that, Ruthie. Have you tried Dalia's Little Ear cookies?"

"Not one time, but twice," Ruth continued, looking at her sternly, clearly not accepting Aunt Em's defense of a faulty memory.

Aunt Em shrugged. "For the painting."

"You want him to buy one of my paintings?"

Aunt Em grew very busy untangling her amber necklace from the top button of her jacket.

"But he certainly has opinions." Ruth gave her empty bowl to a young woman picking up plates and glasses. "Waltzed in my front door this morning with some weak excuse about you sending him and started playing art critic. Hah."

"Was he right?" Aunt Em asked calmly.

Now it was Ruth's turn to shrug. "He might have stumbled onto a couple of insights. I don't know how he did it, though. Law of averages, I guess"

"I thought so."

Ruth's eyebrows rose. "Why would you think live-by-the-books Carter Houston would have opinions about *any* art, let alone mine?"

"Because of his painting."

"What painting?"

"In his office. I saw it when we were there."

Ruth relaxed. "Oh, Em, the painting on the floor? He said he'd thought of hanging it up but then he decided not to. It really wasn't his style. At least he has enough insight to understand that."

"He painted it."

"He painted it," Ruth echoed, her voice dropping flat with shock. "Carter? Why on earth would you believe that?"

"His name was on it, so I asked him. He paints in his house. All the time, in a..." She waved her hands as if to part invisible curtains to find the word. "...room."

"A studio?" Ruth supplied, still sounding incredulous, then asked, each word emphasized, "Carter - Houston - has - a - studio? *Our* Carter Houston?"

Aunt Em appeared inordinately pleased with herself. "We had a good long talk, the detective and me. He wanted to be a painter but nobody bought his paintings, so he had to be a policeman."

Ruth closed her mouth, opened and closed it, her expression stunned, and sat back in her chair, her face a brown study.

Dalia leaned between Helma and Aunt Em, holding the photos from the funeral. "Have you seen the pictures, Emily?" she asked. "Anna asked me to show them to you. She said you'd like to see all of her family."

"I've seen them," Helma said, trying to forestall an exhibition of the ghoulish photos.

"Not me." Aunt Em reached for the glossy 8 x 10 pictures. She pulled the first one close to her face, rejecting Dalia's helpful suggestion that she name each person for her. "I only want to see Rimas." At the next long paper-covered table, Anna watched her, an expectant expression on her face. Aunt Em waved the photos toward her.

"You asked about Everett?" Dalia said to Helma. "He just came in. He's sitting by the coffee pot."

Ruth leaned behind Aunt Em and nudged Helma's shoulder. "Do you think it's true?" she asked in a low voice. "About Carter painting?"

"I don't know. It sounded true, but..."

Ruth looked meaningfully at Aunt Em and nodded. "Maybe not quite as true as it sounds. A permutation thereof, perhaps."

Helma agreed, trying and failing to visualize the tidy detective in a painter's smock standing in front of an easel and applying paint, in colors as gaudy as Ruth's, to a canvas.

She rose from the table to refill her cup from the tea carafe, which sat next to the coffee, leaving Ruth sitting beside Aunt Em, hands lax on the paper tablecloth, a faraway look on her face.

"Hello," she said to Everett, who sat in front of a plate that held only a smear of sour cream.

He squinted up at her. "Ah, the librarian. You gave me good books."

"You're very welcome. Are you interested in the Russian Revolution?"

"Verifying old stories, that's all. You're Em's daughter?"

"Niece. Bruno told me he helps you sometimes."

"That boy." Everett laughed. "He's a piece of work."

"What do you mean?"

"He reminds me of a friend I had long ago. He lived in the crack between bold and illegal. His future looked shaky." He weighed his hands. "Prisoner or President."

"And Bruno lives that that?" Helma asked.

"He does, he does. Prisoner or President."

"Maybe he has good friends who will help guide him," Helma suggested, allowing her voice to rise in a question.

"I don't know his friends," Everett said. "But so far, so good."

"And what happened to your friend of long ago?" Helma asked. "What did he become?"

"Ah, George? He died." And after a perfect pause, Everett added, "In prison."

"Have you thought any more about joining?" Dalia Stone asked as she poured tea into Helma's cup.

"No," she said honestly. Helma only joined groups under duress. "But the organization means a great deal to my aunt." She peered around the room for Bruno, but couldn't locate him.

Returning to the table, she came to an abrupt stop, holding her tea high, waiting for a young girl to dodge past chasing a pudgy baby, and sat down beside Aunt Em who was frowning over one of the photos. She turned and gripped Helma's wrist, spilling Helma's tea.

"Wilhelmina," she whispered as Helma hurriedly set down the cup and used her napkin to wipe the table and her hand. "Wilhelmina," Aunt Em repeated, and Helma folded the napkin and turned her attention to Aunt Em. She was tapping the photo, a look of shock on her face. "This is him."

"Rimas?" Helma asked. Had Aunt Em already forgotten that Rimas had died?

Aunt Em vigorously shook her head, still tapping. "No. This is the robber."

Aunt Em's fingertip touched the photo of the family gathered around the casket. "Which one?" Helma asked.

One of the men in the photograph, John, stood at the food table, ladling glops of onion sauce over a potato.

"Him." It was the younger man, the grandson, who'd captured Aunt Em's attention. Helma took the photo and raised it closer to her face, picturing the suited young man in jeans, his hair uncombed, and in a hurry.

She recognized him. It was the young man who'd dashed in with the funeral photos when Helma had delivered Aunt Em's thank-you card to the Lithuanian Club. Helma quickly surveyed the room. He wasn't present.

"Are you sure?" she asked Aunt Em.

"Of course I am sure. I remember the way his ears..." She made flapping motions beside her own ears. "A good Lithuanian boy, too." She glanced toward Anna, who was being served a slice of apple pie with whipped cream on top from the banquet table, and her eyes took on a sudden gleam. "It will break his family's heart that they have a robber in their bosom." She nodded. "And maybe a murderer...break their hearts."

"Mmm?" Ruth said from the other side of Aunt Em, her eyes still distant.

"I'll find out where he is," Helma told Aunt Em. She gently removed the photo from her aunt's clutched fingers and carried it to Dalia Stone, who was straightening a stack of napkins in preparation of storing them in a plastic container.

"My aunt believes she recognizes this man," she told Dalia. "I think you told me his name was Tony and he's Rimas's..."

Dalia frowned at the photo. "Oh yes. That's Antanas: Tony. He's Rimas's grandson. They were very close." She leaned toward Helma, dropping her voice. "His parents had...problems, and Rimas practically raised the boy for the first twelve years of his life. He was devastated by Rimas's death."

"Is he here?" Helma asked.

Dalia shook her head. "He just left. Bruno drove him to the airport for a flight back to Chicago." She looked up at the clock, "Bruno should be back any minute. Have you seen Bruno?" she asked the woman helping her clear the tables, who said she hadn't.

"*Now* where did he go?" Dalia asked – rhetorically, Helma believed.

Helma thought. In the library, on several occasions she'd helped someone who was flying out of Bellehaven. There were several flights a day to Seattle, and from there passengers connected to the major airlines.

"He departed from Bellehaven?" she verified.

"That's what I understood. I hope Bruno didn't have a crazy idea to drive him all the way to Seattle. I need him here."

"Thank you."

There was no telephone in the club, so Helma asked Ruth for the loan of her cell phone.

"Sure," Ruth told her, fishing around in her voluminous bag. "It might be dead, though."

The battery icon was nearly empty, but Helma carried it to the vestibule and called the number she was most familiar with: the library's.

Glory answered in her girlish voice. While Helma definitely did not try to disguise her voice, she maintained a cool, business-like demeanor. "What time is the next flight to Seattle from the Bellehaven airport?"

It was no use. "Oh, Helma, are you taking a trip? You're not listed on the roster as taking time off."

"Do you have the time of departure?" she asked.

"Sure. In thirty minutes. Where are you going? Is Wayne going with— "

"Thank you," Helma said, and ended the call, already on her way back to the meeting room.

"I have to leave," she told Ruth and Aunt Em as she reached for her coat, hindered at first by slipping her arm into the wrong sleeve. "Ruth, can you take Aunt Em home in a taxi?"

Ruth sat up straight, blinking and returning to the present. "Why? What's happening? What am I missing?"

"I told Helma who the robber is," Aunt Em explained to Ruth, "and now she is hot on his trail."

"Oh, we definitely can't miss this." Ruth stood and helped Aunt Em rise with one hand while she draped Aunt Em's coat over her shoulder with the other.

"Please," Helma tried. "He's about to catch a flight from the Bellehaven airport. There's no reason for you to—"

"Don't waste time arguing. We're coming, right, Em?"

"Let's go like Billy Bejeezus," Aunt Em quoted from one of her favorite John Wayne movies.

Helma remembered her father saying, "You have to know when to fish or cut bait," and gave up, warning the two women, "Then we have to hurry. The flight leaves in twenty-five minutes."

Hurrying had an entirely different meaning when one was in the company of a nearly ninety-year-old woman. "What if I just pick her up and carry her?" Ruth murmured to Helma as they escorted Aunt Em in a maddeningly slow fashion toward

Helma's car, one on either side of her, a single deliberate step at a time.

Helma seriously considered the option, then shook her head. "A minute or so won't make any difference," she told Ruth.

"Do you actually believe that?" Ruth asked.

"No," Helma admitted, and gasped as Ruth *did* pick up Aunt Em in her arms, carrying her like an oversized child, moving so fast Helma broke into a run to keep up. Aunt Em smiled benignly in Ruth's arms, as comfortable as if this were a mode of travel she engaged in regularly.

CHAPTER 19

A Small Misunderstanding

Helma chose a route along the west side of Bellehaven, following streets with fewer traffic lights. After she and Wayne were married she'd ask him if it were really true that the police didn't apprehend drivers who drove within five miles over the speed limit. She nudged her Buick to four miles over the limit, obediently dropping back when they passed through a school zone.

"If he gets away, will you follow him to Chicago?" Aunt Em asked from the back seat.

"Helma will pursue him to the ends of the Earth," Ruth promised her, and Aunt Em settled into her seat, saying, "I thought so."

"If Rimas's grandson is the robber, Aunt Em, did you met him before the robbery?" Helma asked as she passed – despite Ruth's "Yeep!" – a slow-moving pickup with plenty of room to pull back into her lane before the oncoming car.

"I can't remember." Aunt Em's voice was uncertain. "Maybe I saw him with Rimas? Or Anna? If I did, now it's gone."

There were rules about parking in front of the airport, and Helma had no intention of breaking any of them. She pulled her Buick to the curb of the "Loading Zone," switched on her hazard lights, and stepped out. Any official determined to enforce the law could easily see that Aunt Em needed assistance.

"You help Aunt Em," she told Ruth. "I'll stop the plane."

As the electronic doors parted in front of her, Helma heard Aunt Em say, "Wilhelmina can stop a plane?" and Ruth respond, "If anybody can, she's the one. C'mon. Let's watch her."

Passengers at the small Bellehaven airport were still required to exit the terminal and walk across the tarmac to a roll-away staircase to board their plane, and through the plate glass windows Helma saw a line of passengers snaking from the security area to the rolling staircase of a small jet, an MD-80. She scanned the passengers, then the lobby area for Bruno or Tony, but didn't spot either man.

"Excuse me," she said, stepping in front of a woman wrestling an obviously oversized and overweight suitcase toward the ticket counter, "but this is an emergency."

The woman scowled and actually shoved her rolling red suitcase into Helma's path, blocking her way. "Your emergency is not my emergency."

"You might consider this your emergency if a dangerous person were on your airplane," Helma told her.

"Ma'am," the female airline employee at the counter called out, but before Helma had a chance to explain the urgency of the situation to the woman, two uniformed men stood beside her, one on each side, pressing uncomfortably close.

The woman with the luggage gave a needlessly satisfied, "Hah," and pushed ahead, leaving Helma standing between the security guards.

"Is there a problem, ma'am?" one of the men asked in a conversational manner.

"A man who may have robbed my aunt and committed murder is boarding that airplane." Since there was only one airplane being boarded she felt it unnecessary to signify which plane.

The two security men considered her calmly, one of them looking out at the plane with three people ascending the stairway and two still waiting on the tarmac. "Have you spoken to the police?" the other one asked. There was no mistaking the indulgence in his voice.

"There hasn't been time, but you can't allow the plane to depart with him aboard. His name is Tony—Antanas Klimas. My aunt—"

"Let's step in here," the first guard, an older man with a gap between his front teeth suggested, bowing her toward an open door behind the ticket counter. "You can tell us all about it."

"Hey!" It was Ruth, entering the terminal and pulling, nearly dragging, Aunt Em along with her. "Leave her alone."

The guard who'd beckoned Helma toward the room told the other guard, who appeared younger and more eager to enforce whatever he had the power to enforce, "Invite her to come join us, would you?" and motioned toward Ruth.

"My aunt," Helma said. "Don't leave my aunt alone in the terminal. She becomes...confused." She switched to her silver-dime voice. "And I *am* accompanying you. Please remove your hand."

He didn't remove his hand, although his grip did slightly relax. The room he escorted her into was bare, reminding Helma of the rooms used in the police station to question suspicious citizens, and which she'd unfortunately experienced herself: nothing in it but a small table and four chairs beneath a sign advising the traveler to never leave baggage unattended.

Ruth stumbled in behind her, sputtering and cranky, with the other security guard holding his hand behind her back as if he were acting the gentleman. "You think I'm going to bomb a plane or something? You're crazy."

"I'd advise you not to use those terms, ma'am."

"Which 'terms'? Bomb, or crazy?"

"Either one."

"It's a free country. You can't arrest me for saying words that are in the dictionary," Ruth protested as she dropped into the chair beside Helma.

"I'm afraid we can."

Ruth looked at Helma for confirmation, her face red, and Helma nodded. "They can."

"What kind of——" Ruth began.

"Where's my aunt?" Helma interrupted.

"Waiting in the lobby," the guard said. "She's fine. Let's discuss the murderer you claim is on the plane."

Unmistakably, behind them, Helma heard the revving of airplane engines. "I suppose being on the airplane is as good as being apprehended," she conceded. "You can detain him when the plane lands in Seattle."

"If there's a reason to, we will. Now, can you explain why you believe he's a murderer?"

"My aunt was robbed by two men," she explained, speaking slowly, drawing on patience she didn't feel. "And in the robbery, one of the robbers was killed, presumably by his accomplice. Only a few minutes ago my aunt recognized the other robber's photo, and we discovered he was about to leave Bellehaven by airplane."

"Did you see him?"

"No."

The security guards' eyes briefly met.

"You wouldn't let her get near the plane," Ruth reminded them. "How was she supposed to see him?

Ruth wasn't helping. "You're not helping, Ruth," Helma said.

"I am too. Why don't you ask her aunt? Bring her in here and she'll explain."

The dominant security guard nodded to the other one, who left the room.

"Can we talk about——" the remaining security guard began.

"Not until her aunt gets here," Ruth said, and clamped her mouth closed.

They sat in silence, waiting for what seemed an unreasonably long time. Helma began to shift uncomfortably in her chair. The guard had claimed he'd left Aunt Em in the middle of the lobby. Certainly she was plainly visible. Helma hoped she hadn't wandered off—or resisted the guard.

Finally, after enough time for Ruth to work her way through a series of huffs and puffs, and for Helma to mentally recite a favorite childhood poem that began, "The gingham dog and the calico cat side by side on the table sat," the guard returned, with Aunt Em leaning on him, her hand tucked into the crook of his arm. Aunt Em was smiling.

"Em," Ruth said. "Tell the guards about your robbery."

Aunt Em's eyes flew open. Her mouth formed an O. "I was robbed?" she asked in horror. "When?"

CHAPTER 20

Pulled from the Sky

"Please call the Bellehaven police and ask for Carter Houston," Helma requested. "I will speak no more about this situation until he's informed of our presence here."

"Ditto," Ruth said, making zipping motions across her lips.

"I'll tell you everything," Aunt Em said agreeably, but neither security guard took her up on the offer. In fact, neither paid her much attention.

The guard was reaching for the telephone when a knock sounded on the office door.

"Yes?" the young guard gruffly called out.

The door opened and a voice inquired, "Can I help?"

They looked up to see Carter Houston step into the room. A sheen of perspiration covered his forehead. He breathed in gasps, as if he'd been running. And most telling, his tie was askew.

"How'd you get here?" Ruth asked.

"I called him," Aunt Em said proudly. "I have his personal phone number."

"You wrote it down?" Helma asked her.

"I memorized it," Aunt Em said. "I can still memorize." She paused. "If I try hard enough." She paused again. "Sometimes."

Ruth looked sharply at Aunt Em. "You memorized his personal phone number so you could send him to my house to look at my paintings?"

"It was my own good idea," Aunt Em admitted proudly.

"I'll take over now," Carter told the security guards, reaching out with surprising smoothness to shake their hands. He waited until they'd both stepped back against the wall, arms folded like bookends before he sat down and took his notebook from his pocket. Ruth watched through half-narrowed eyes, as if Carter had just proven himself to be a confounding creature she hadn't believed existed, instead of her favorite target for tormenting.

He smiled at Aunt Em. "You told me you recognized the burglar in a photograph?"

Aunt Em nodded. "It is Rimas Klimas's grandson. I saw his photograph, with the casket. Anna was so proud of him. Tsk, tsk."

"And you're sure he's the same man you confronted in your apartment?"

Aunt Em nodded again, more confidently. "Such a shame."

"Now that you've seen his picture, do you remember more details of the robbery?"

Aunt Em's face went still. She lowered her head and gazed down at her hands. "He stole it," she said and her voice caught. "It's gone."

"What is, Aunt Em?" Helma asked, bending down to look into Aunt Em's face. "What's gone?"

"It doesn't matter now," she whispered. But obviously it did.

Carter touched Aunt Em's shoulder. "I'm going to bring the plane back. Will you identify him for us? We can arrange it so he won't see you."

"Like a two-way mirror?" Aunt Em asked, raising her head. "Like on television?"

"If you want, of course."

"I want to look him in the eye, chin to chin," she said, jabbing a finger at the chair opposite her.

Ruth was uncharacteristically silent, studying Carter intensely, especially his hands. When he left the room, she said in a distant voice, "He has cobalt blue under his fingernails."

The recalled plane landed, taxiing down the runway and lumbering to a stop a far distance from the terminal. Two police cars accompanied by a fire truck waited alongside the runway as if the plane might explode. Lights flashed.

Wayne Gallant joined them in the small room, first acknowledging Helma and briefly touching her shoulder, then pulling a chair next to Aunt Em. "So you're going to identify the robber for us?" he asked her in a jovial voice, taking her hand.

"I will do that," she said simply.

It wasn't long before Carter and a policewoman Helma recognized as Camella escorted Tony into the room and sat him opposite Aunt Em. He was tall and lean, with dark hair, and his left eyebrow was ragged, as if long ago it had been torn. Far from defiant, as might have been expected from a criminal on the run, he instead appeared wide-eyed and troubled. His hands were cuffed behind his back, forcing him to sit leaning his upper body forward.

Helma immediately recognized him as the young man who'd been in such a hurry to deliver the funeral photos to Dalia and be gone, the man in the photograph peering gravely down at Rimas, who Dalia claimed had been "devastated" by his grandfather's death.

Aunt Em gazed at him for a long time before she finally spoke. "Why did you take it all?" she asked.

He lowered his head and a lock of dark hair fell forward. "I'm sorry."

Ruth opened her mouth and Wayne signaled her to be silent. She shrugged.

"My father, my Papa, gave it to me, as the oldest," Aunt Em continued. "There is no more."

Camella touched Aunt Em's shoulder. "Can I get you a glass of water?" she whispered in her soothing voice. Aunt Em shook her head, but patted Camella's hand.

Tony kept his head down, rocking a little in his chair. "I needed it for my grandfather," he said in a low voice. "The last time I saw him I promised him, but I didn't have time. I wasn't prepared. I didn't really expect him to...die."

Aunt Em harrumphed. "Nobody gets out alive," sounding like another of her favorite John Wayne characters.

Helma was finally beginning to understand. "The *Stelmužė* box actually does open, doesn't it?"

Aunt Em unclasped her patent leather purse and pulled out the *Stelmužė* box. It was wrapped in a white handkerchief with black embroidered edges. She withdrew the box and set it on the table where they could all see it, her hand lingering on its surface.

The box had been so integral to Aunt Em's surroundings: in her house, then her apartment, that Helma had taken it for granted. Now, in this stark setting, the delicate blade marks that covered it surface formed light and shadow of exotic intensity.

Aunt Em reached into her purse again and removed a hat pin that Helma knew she always carried, "for safety."

"I will show you." Slowly, holding her breath to steady her hands, she turned the box so a narrow end faced her and inserted the pointed end of the hat pin into the center of one of the geometric designs.

Nothing happened until she slid the top like a match box cover. And there, revealed before them was a small compartment.

Aunt Em had been correct. There was nothing inside.

Helma turned her head from Aunt Em to Antanas, asking both of them. "Was there sand inside the box? Sand from Lithuania?"

Aunt Em nodded. "To be buried with. I dusted some in each of my brothers' and sisters' coffins. I saved a little for myself..." She shrugged.

"You broke into my mother and aunt's apartment to steal... sand?" Helma asked Tony. "You killed somebody for *sand*?"

"I didn't kill anybody," he burst out, finally raising his head. His eyes were red. "He – Chip – was supposed to watch the hallway for me, that's all. Nothing else, I told him that. Nothing else. I had to do it in broad daylight because the funeral was only a few hours away. Chip started sticking things in his pockets. I already had the box and I told him to put the other stuff back, and...." He leaned back as far as his bound hands would allow him, breathing with frightening rapidity.

Helma changed the tenor of the scene. "And so every grain of Aunt Em's sand was buried with your grandfather?" she clarified in the same neutral voice she'd once used to calm a library patron who'd broken the library's new sixteen-inch illuminated floor globe.

He nodded glumly and took a deep breath. "I only meant to sprinkle a few grains in my grandfather's coffin, but one of the funeral guys walked in while I was doing it and I jerked my hand. It all fell into the casket."

"Why not just use regular dirt from a sandbox or dig it out from under a tree?" Ruth asked. "It's not like your grandfather would know the difference."

Both Tony and Aunt Em looked at Ruth with evident horror on their faces. Ruth raised her hands. "Okay, okay. I get it. Doesn't work."

"Had you and your accomplice worked together before?" Wayne asked.

"He wasn't an accomplice, just some guy I heard about."

"Who from?"

He pressed his lips together and looked down.

"You knew him, then?"

"No," Tony mumbled. "I asked around. A guy who knew people told me to ask another guy, and..." he trailed off.

"Did you threaten Chip Block with the carving knife," Carter asked, "until finally you forced him out the window?"

Tony's eyes darted to Aunt Em so fast that Helma reached out her hand as if to protect her. He and Aunt Em locked eyes and she calmly gazed back at him.

"The knife," he repeated, as if trying to remember, still looking at Aunt Em.

They all sat silently, waiting for him to continue. Finally he said quietly to Aunt Em, "I'm sorry about the dirt. I would have returned any that was left. I'd planned to take a few grains and give back the box. You never would have known."

He broke eye contact with her and spoke directly to the chief. "I threatened Chip with the carving knife. He was taking the TV and I told him to put it back, but he wouldn't so..." He frowned. "So I grabbed the knife and told him I was going to slash his throat."

"And he jumped out the window," Ruth finished. "Just like that?"

"Well, he backed up," Tony explained in a halting voice, "Until there was no more room. I had the knife, see?"

"Why did you send Helma her mother's wedding ring?" Wayne asked while at the same time Ruth muttered to Helma, "The kid's lying."

Helma knew he was, too. But somehow, without words, an agreement, maybe actually a bargain, had been made between Tony and Aunt Em.

"I picked up the ring off the floor after Chip... fell," Tony told Wayne. "I didn't mean to steal anything."

"You're making a pretty fine distinction there," Carter commented.

"I was in a hurry to get out of the apartment and I forgot I had the ring. I admit I intended to take the box, okay? But I was going to put it back. I only wanted a few grains."

"How did you know she had Lithuanian sand?" Wayne asked, nodding toward Aunt Em.

He didn't answer.

"Did someone in your family tell you?" Helma asked. "Perhaps someone who'd seen Aunt Em's *Stelmužė* box? Your aunt?"

He didn't answer her, either.

Aunt Em watched Tony intently, on her face a sorrowful expression.

"We're taking you to the station," Wayne told the young man. "You have the right to..."

They all sat silently listening to the chief read Tony his Miranda rights while Tony sat with head bowed and eyes closed. As Wayne finished, Aunt Em said, "It sounds like a prayer."

"Amen," Ruth commented.

"Could you take Ruth and my aunt home?" Helma asked Carter Houston. "There's something I have to do."

Wayne paused in directing Tony's removal and frowned at her. "Does it have anything to do with the robbery? Is this a police concern?"

"No. Of course not."

"I'll come with you," Ruth told Helma. Then she looked at Carter and hesitated. Her nose wrinkled. "Well, maybe I'll go with Em and Carter to make sure he doesn't get lost."

"You'd be welcome, Miss Winthrop," Carter said, and cleared his throat, then cleared it again. "If you'd like to accompany us, that is."

Camella was the last to leave the room. Helma waited for her beside the door. "I want to thank you for the kindness you've shown Aunt Em."

"You're welcome," the policewoman responded coolly.

Helma held out her hand and smiled. Camella took it and they politely shook, but Helma thought she saw the corners of Camella's mouth rise a fraction.

In front of the Lithuanian Club, Dalia's son, Bruno shoved a cardboard box in the back of a station wagon. Helma climbed out of her car. Bruno turned, saw her and began edging toward the corner of the building.

"Bruno," she called. "May we speak for a moment?"

He slouched back toward her, reluctance in every step. Drizzle sparkled on his shoulders. Helma felt it already clinging to her hair. "Yeah? What?"

"The police have arrested Antanas Klimas."

"So?" he said, looking over her shoulder at nothing.

"He hasn't given them your name yet, but I don't know how..." She thought of gangster movies, "...how heavy they'll lean on him."

"I didn't do anything."

"Did you know my aunt had dirt from Lithuania?"

He glanced at her sharply and then lowered his head again, kicking at the gravel. "I didn't," he said, striking his fist into his palm. "I didn't know what he'd planned."

She believed him. "Your mother said you're gifted at connecting people with what they want, such as Aunt Em's 999, and Baltic mementos for the nostalgic. I assume that means you're as good at connecting people looking for people to assist them, as well. Did you know Chip Block, too?"

He mumbled.

"I beg your pardon."

Bruno glared toward the street. "I heard about him. I might have mentioned Chip's name to Tony, I don't remember."

Helma held out a business card. "Take this in case you do recall how Tony and Chip connected. It's the chief of police's card. I don't believe you actually committed a crime, but it's far easier to come forward with information than to have the police..." she thought of the movies again. "...hunt you down like a dog."

He didn't answer, but he took the card without meeting her eyes.

"I met a man who believes you have the qualities of a presidential candidate," she told him.

He nodded, and still didn't raise his head.

As she drove away, in her rearview mirror, Helma saw Bruno standing behind his mother's car, peering down at Wayne's card as if it were speaking to him.

Helma crossed the parking lot to the Bayside Arms, a spring in her step, lightened by the sense of criminal mysteries unwinding and order returning. She heard a noise and looked up to see TNT standing in the drizzle on the steps, a slicker draped over his clothes, the hood covering his head. As soon as he spotted her, he hurried down the steps toward her, his face dead serious.

Helma's heart thudded. Her steps slowed. Something had happened.

"I've been waiting for ye, girly girl," TNT said, reaching for her arm. "Your mother sent me. Your aunt's suffered a wee collapse."

CHAPTER 21

The Speed of Life

TNT drove, and Helma couldn't have said what streets they traveled or whether he obeyed the traffic rules. Even if she'd looked out the window of his Jeep, she wouldn't have recognized the scenery.

"She was in the policeman's car," TNT explained to her, "on her way back to her apartment, so they took her straight to the hospital. Couldn't have got her there any faster if they'd had an ambulance," he reassured her.

Except in an ambulance, Helma thought, they could have begun treatment immediately. Moments counted.

"Your mother and I were at her apartment, so Ruthie phoned us first. Your mother, bless her, wouldn't let them phone you. She told me to come here to tell you in person."

"Ruth was with her?" Helma asked, remembering that of course Ruth was with her, with Carter, a niggling feeling of sad and glad intermixing. She was relieved Aunt Em hadn't been alone. Yet, *Helma* should have been with her.

She asked what she'd been avoiding so far. "How serious is it?"

TNT cast a kindly look at her, as if he'd been about to shake his head and decided against it. "It's too soon to tell."

She jumped out of TNT's Jeep before he could park, belatedly realizing she'd never fastened her seatbelt, and hearing him shout after her, "Room 324!"

Helma raced up the three flights of stairs to the third floor, seeing first of all as she pushed open the fire door, Wayne Gallant facing her. Without another thought, she stepped into his arms and he held her, saying against her hair, "I was waiting for you. I knew you'd take the stairs."

"They're faster," she said and swallowed, fighting the shake in her voice. "Is she…"

"She's comfortable right now. It looks like a stroke. Not a bad one, but…"

Helma already knew from research she'd helped a woman find in the library that in the very elderly and frail, one stroke was often followed by a second. She nodded and Wayne took her elbow, guiding her toward room 324.

Aunt Em reclined against a hill of pillows, wearing a pink cotton hospital gown with tiny flowers on it. She was pale, her eyes dreamy.

"Daisies," Aunt Em murmured when she saw Helma looking at the hospital gown, plucking at the fabric, "My favorite." Her voice was thick, one side of her mouth drooped.

Lillian fussed around the bed, tugging at blankets and pillows, really changing nothing. "Now, Em," she spoke in an irritated voice. "Just lie still and rest. You'll be fine if you mind the doctor's orders, just fine. You only have to listen and obey, do you hear me?"

TNT gently touched Lillian's shoulder and slipped his arm around her. Instantly, Helma's mother sank against him, looking smaller and frailer herself.

Helma leaned over the bed, careful of the tubing, and kissed Aunt Em's forehead. Anything she could say sounded trite, so she only murmured, "Hello, Aunt Em."

Aunt Em heaved a sigh. "Wilhelmina," she whispered, entreaty in her voice.

"What do you need?"

Aunt Em beckoned her closer. Helma leaned her ear toward Aunt Em's mouth. "Get them out of here," she whispered. "All but you."

"I'll try."

"No," Aunt Em said emphatically. "Do it."

Helma straightened and looked around the room. Besides Aunt Em, six people stood or sat in various poses, all eyes focused on Aunt Em.

"Excuse me," she said to no one in particular and slipped out of Aunt Em's room. She walked down the hall to the nurses' station and asked, "Will you be administering personal care to my aunt soon?"

The nurse looked up at the clock behind the desk. "On the hour," she frowned questioningly at Helma. "Unless she needs us now?"

"That'll be fine," Helma told her.

When she returned to Aunt Em's room, she paused in the doorway and announced, "The nurses will be administering personal care to Aunt Em soon. We can wait in the cafeteria."

They all tiptoed out, Helma last. At the end of the hall, she stopped. "Go ahead, I left my purse in Aunt Em's room."

Ruth, who, curiously, was walking beside Carter Houston, frowned at her. Helma ignored her and hurried back to Aunt Em's room.

At first she thought Aunt Em was asleep, but as Helma pulled a chair closer to the bed, she opened her eyes. "Will you help me, Wilhelmina?"

"Any way I can," Helma assured her as she smoothed the light blanket around Aunt Em's shoulders.

"Will you marry the chief?"

"Of course." Aunt Em had forgotten her engagement already. "Do it tomorrow."

"Tomorrow?" Helma repeated.

"I want to see it."

"You'll be there, Aunt Em, whenever we plan it."

"Tomorrow," Aunt Em repeated. "Now go do what you have to do. Tell your mother to come. I'll wait here."

CHAPTER 22

A Slight Change of Plans

"What? Why do we have to rush everything? That old fool thinks she's going to die, doesn't she? She always has to make herself the center of attention." Lillian stood up from the table in the cafeteria so quickly that her glass tipped and would have fallen if TNT hadn't grabbed it. "Now, Lil," he soothed.

"No. I mean it. What about Helma's dress? Mister Dubois? All the plans?"

"Wayne and I have only been planning to marry for a few days," Helma reminded her. "We haven't had time to make any plans."

"She's ruining everything," Lillian cried, and tears spilled from her eyes. "Rushing it all like this, like it's some kind of emergency."

TNT awkwardly patted her, saying "Now, don't fash, Lil," but she shrugged off his hand.

"I like it," Ruth suddenly said, speaking only to Lillian. "You know how long you've been waiting for Helma to capitulate to the chief's charms." She glanced apologetically at Wayne. "What we'll get is a done deal, right before our very eyes. No time for Helma to get all wishy-washy and claim some library emergency to postpone the wedding. Nobody's getting any younger around here."

"It's not the way I wanted it," Lillian protested.

Ruth actually took Lillian's hand between her own, her fore-head close to Lillian's. "Em really loves you," she said quietly. "You're her nearest and dearest."

Lillian wiped her eyes and made a motion that was almost a nod. After a few moments, she spoke in a tentative voice, "I suppose if it's what Em really wants, we'll just have to do it her way." She straightened her shoulders. "I might be able to use some of the plans I've already made— later." She glanced at TNT and actually blushed. "What about the license?" she asked Helma. "Is there time to get a license before tomorrow?"

Wayne Gallant frowned. "I think we can arrange it." His eyes caught Helma's. A quiver ticked in his jaw. "Tomorrow," he said, smiling but sounding stricken.

Helma nodded. For some reason she couldn't make a single word issue forth from her mouth.

"Okay, guys," Ruth said, standing. "Let's get cracking. This tomorrow is not going to creep in at any petty pace."

"Shakespeare," Carter Houston said, and Ruth laughed as if she were delighted. Helma felt dizzy.

"Come with me," Wayne told her. "We'll go tackle City Hall right now."

"I want to tell Aunt Em first," Helma said. She'd expected to go alone, but Wayne nodded and accompanied her. Not just walking beside her but...together, as if they were a...unit, as if there were no question but they would see Aunt Em together, that from now on there would be no question about several aspects of her life...*their* life.

Aunt Em didn't open her eyes until Helma lightly touched her shoulder, and then she looked between Helma and Wayne, whispering, "Nice."

"We'll be married tomorrow," Helma said, feeling like she was speaking a foreign language. "Here in this room at eleven in the morning."

"Good," she said. "Is good."

Lillian entered the room behind them, TNT still at her side. Aunt Em looked at Lillian. "Now you have work."

"You'd think they'd want fingerprints," Helma commented to Wayne as they left City Hall.

He laughed. "Marriage isn't a crime. Besides, we're both well known around here. Hard to fake our identities."

"Will there be a problem waving the waiting period?" They stepped around a man and woman gazing at a single sheet of paper held between them.

He shook his head. "I'll take care of it. Do you have time to buy a dress? I trust your mother will take care of any other arrangements."

It would be simple, a light suit, she'd decided. "What's going to happen to Tony Klimas?"

He shook his head. "Carter's case. Don't think about it right now."

On the busy sidewalk between City Hall and the library he tipped her chin and kissed her. "I'll call you tonight."

Helma watched him hurry off toward the courthouse. She swallowed. Her almost husband.

It was as if a public announcement had been made when Helma entered the library workroom. George Melville spotted her first. "How's your aunt?" he asked, rubbing a hand through his beard. "And a wedding tomorrow, too?"

"How did you already hear?"

"You know this place. Somebody's cousin works in City Hall who told a pink lady at the hospital whose brother has an overdue library fine and was once arrested by a policeman." He shrugged. "Bittersweet, isn't it?

Helma agreed, it was, and then she was surrounded by Junie, the clerk, Ms. Moon, Eve, even Dutch on the periphery. She couldn't catch her breath. "I only need to pick up my sweater," she said helplessly. "Thank you, thank you."

Safely in her cubicle and folding her sweater, she raised her head to see Glory brushing the end of a red curl across her cheek.

"I didn't think you'd be the first single person to get married around here. I thought it would be somebody younger." The red curl went into the corner of her mouth and she gave a single unmirthful giggle. "Like me."

"I'm sure a future awaits you, Glory," she said, and generously added, "and happiness, too."

Glory frowned. "I don't know. I keep trying, but it doesn't ever work out, you know what I mean?"

Glory's eyes were thoughtful. She wore a pink ribbon in her hair and a childish dress with a princess waist, her legs covered by brightly patterned tights.

"What do you think's wrong with me?" Glory asked, absently snapping the colored beads of her elastic bracelet.

On impulse, Helma unfolded the sweater she'd just folded, reached into the pocket and found Mister Dubois's card. She removed it and held it out to Glory. "I have an appointment with him this afternoon but it's no longer necessary that I keep it. Would you like to go in my place?"

Glory gasped and snatched the card from Helma's fingers. "I'd love to," she breathed, and whirled away.

Helma had an uncanny memory for numbers, even more than names and dates, and she unerringly dialed Mr. Dubois's phone number. "I'd like to ask you a favor," she said after she'd identified herself.

When she hung up it was to see Ruth leaning against Helma's cubicle and glancing toward Glory's cubicle. "What did you do to make her day?"

"Personal care suggestions," Helma said. "What are you doing here? Oh no, is Aunt Em— "

Ruth held up her hand. "She's fine, well, as fine as anybody can be who's stuck in the hospital. I came to take you shopping for the Event."

"There's no reason to, Ruth. I saw a suit at Jane's Fashions I intend to buy."

"Plain Jane's?" Ruth made a Pffft sound. "Not bloody likely. It's your first wedding and, at the rate you make up your mind, it'll be your last. I already called the Bridal Bar and they're spreading out a choice selection for you, even as we speak. Can't do much in the way of alterations at this late date, but I bet we can find something that fits like the proverbial."

"The wedding's in the hospital and I have no intention of wearing a wedding gown."

"What, you afraid you'll get germs on it and won't get to wear it again? You're too late, anyway. I already promised your aunt."

"When?"

"By proxy. Your mother called me. It's either come with me or she's going to pick out an ensemble for you herself, and I guarantee, she's fizzed up to do it. What do you think?"

Either choice smelled of disaster, so Helma chose the least of two bad options. "All right, if we can do it in one hour."

"No problem."

"I need to talk to Ms. Moon first," she told Ruth.

"Go ahead. I'll go see what Dutch is up to."

Ms. Moon sat at her desk, studying an array of sign holders resting on top of a set of blueprints. She looked up at Helma and tapped a bronze rectangle. "This one, I think," she said in a distracted fashion.

"It's very handsome," Helma agreed.

Ms. Moon nodded. "For the shelf-ends in the new library. They're the same patina as the brass knobs on the wall sconces."

"Quite ornate," Helma commented. "I understood we'd be recycling the sign holders from our current shelves."

"Those plain old things?" Ms. Moon said. "Not in my...our, new library. The public expects better."

"The budget..." Helma reminded her delicately.

Ms. Moon waved a hand. "I found a little more funding for... niceties. This money won't be part of the overall budget." She smiled. "It's extra."

Helma took a step closer to Ms. Moon's desk, staying, as TNT always advised, "light on her feet."

"I've been thinking about our local authors' demands regarding the bestseller display," she told Ms. Moon.

The director lifted the brass sign holder and held it in the light of her desk lamp, tipping it so it glinted. "Mmm. Did you settle that little issue?"

"I'm very close."

"Good. Please prepare a report for the next staff meeting."

"I can do that."

Ms. Moon held up a second sign holder, turned it in the light, frowned, and set it down again, brushing at a spot on the blueprints. "Fine," she said in a tone of dismissal, reaching for a silver holder.

"I spoke to a manager at Books & Nicknacks yesterday," Helma told her.

"How nice," said with more impatience than distraction.

"She gave me explanations for the way they arranged their bestseller book displays."

Ms. Moon slowly returned the silver holder to her desk. "Oh?"

"Publishers actually *pay* bookstores to have their books displayed in a prominent location," Helma told her.

Ms. Moon shifted her attention to Helma, folding her hands together on the edge of her desk. "Is that right?"

"It is. It's a form of advertising, the manager told me. Publishers are always looking for new ways to advertise their books. These are economically challenging times for publishers, with all the competition from ebooks and computer technology. They even pay to have a book turned face-out on a shelf."

Ms. Moon watched Helma, eyes sharp but her face neutral. "And you're telling me this because...?"

"I found it very interesting, especially since our library's bestsellers and displays are a subject of contention with our regional authors right now."

Ms. Moon didn't move.

"I'm surprised how many of the books on the library's new bestseller table are published by the same publisher," Helma continued. "Have you noticed?"

"There aren't that many active publishers anymore," Ms. Moon waved toward her own bookshelves, as if to illustrate her point. "They're all conglomerates."

Helma nodded. "Big business. Acting as big businesses must: studying their bottom line, investing in ways to advance their sales, such as advertising. The more the public is exposed to their products..."

"What a coincidence." Ms. Moon coughed. "Interestingly enough, I've recently wondered if our bestseller table is an efficient use of our limited space."

"Have you thought of a more varied display?" Helma suggested. "One that included local authors. And without multiple copies of bestsellers?"

The director leaned back in her swivel chair and closed her eyes for a long moment. She pushed her sign holder samples into a shiny heap. "That might better serve our mission as a public library," she said in a faint voice.

Helma smiled. "I'll be happy to arrange the changes for you—and explain your thinking to the authors."

"Thank you."

As Helma turned to leave, Ms. Moon added, "Since the subject is now settled, there won't be any need for you to make a report at the staff meeting."

"That's agreeable."

"Nor to anyone else."

"Of course not," Helma assured her.

Helma Zukas gave herself up to it. In one hour she walked out of the Bridal Bar with a receipt in her hand, an astronomical charge on her credit card, and a promise of delivery in the morning of a dress she couldn't remember and all the accoutrements Ruth and the clerk considered necessary and which Helma had barely noticed, except to demur when Ruth somehow discovered among all the chaste garters a red garter with an obscene charm attached to it.

"Now I'm supposed to deliver you to the command center in your Aunt Em's hospital room," Ruth said, and began humming, "Here Comes the Bride."

Wayne sat in a chair tucked into the alcove four doors down from Aunt Em's hospital room.

"Hiding out?" Ruth asked him.

"More like staying out of the way." His eyes sagged. He looked overwhelmed. "Your mother..."

"Say no more," Ruth told him. "You guys go in. I'll wait out here."

Wayne stood, reaching for Helma's hand. He took a deep breath and squeezed it before they entered Aunt Em's room.

Helma had expected her mother to be present, and she was, but when Lillian saw Helma and Wayne, she rose from her chair beside Aunt Em's bed, gave Aunt Em a quick hug and said, "I'll be waiting down the hall."

"Ruth's in the alcove near the nurses' station," Helma told her as she took her mother's chair beside Aunt Em's bed. "You could join her."

"I could," her mother said.

Aunt Em was drowsy and Helma thought she'd probably had more activity today, on a day when she'd collapsed, than on any normal day in the past three years.

"This is your wedding present," Aunt Em patted a package wrapped in silver paper that rested on the bed beside her. "Open it now."

Helma looked up at Wayne who nodded, and began to carefully undo the taped ends.

"A present should be torn into, Wilhelmina, not opened like it is a bomb."

She tore off the final corner and exposed a cardboard box decorated with glossy embossed writing. It was a bottle of 999, the Green Nines variety. "I only took one sip," Aunt Em told her.

"Thank you, Aunt Em, but..."

"The rest of the present is under the bottle."

Helma lifted out the bottle and handed it to Wayne, whose eyebrows raised as he read the alcoholic content on the ornate label. A square white envelope lay in the bottom of the box. "I hope your mother did it right," Aunt Em said.

The envelope was addressed to "Police Chief and Mrs. Wayne Gallant"—in her mother's hand—and it was glued closed. "Open it, open it," Aunt Em encouraged her. Wayne gave Helma his keys and she chose a brass key that said "Do Not Duplicate" on it to slit the envelope.

Inside were two tickets to Vilnius, Lithuania.

"For your honeymoon," Aunt Em's face was warm with a wide, tilted smile. "You should know your roots."

"Oh, Aunt Em."

"Is good?"

"More than good, much more," Helma told her.

"I'm tired, Wilhelmina," Aunt Em said, closing her eyes. "Tomorrow."

And that fast, she drifted off. A snore escaped her lips. Helma and Wayne each kissed her forehead and tiptoed out.

At the door of her apartment, Wayne folded Helma into his arms. "I've got to go back to the station. There's a young man named Bruno who's insisting on talking to me," he told her.

"I believe he may have shown bad judgment, but I'm not sure he committed a crime," Helma said.

"If that's true, he doesn't have much to worry about. Until tomorrow."

"Tomorrow," Helma repeated.

"And tomorrow night," he cleared his throat. "I thought we could stay in Vancouver, but I'm guessing you'd like to be closer to your aunt."

"I would."

"Then. . ." His shoulders relaxed. "Is this all too much, Helma? It's happening faster than we anticipated. And if you'd rather, tomorrow night can wait until. . .until you're more comfortable."

She touched his chest, feeling the slow, steady beat of his heart through her palm. "I think. . ." she cleared her throat. "I think I'd be very comfortable spending tomorrow night at your house."

Twice during the long night Helma phoned the hospital. "Resting comfortably," she was told both times. She spent most of the night sitting in her living room under the greeny-gold gaze of Boy Cat Zukas, who sat curled in his basket, opening his eyes whenever she moved as she struggled to catalog the day's events into a more logical order. The day had transpired in a whirlwind, and every move she'd made to control it had been swept out of her hands. Murder and marriage, stolen sand, Aunt Em. She shivered, and Boy Cat Zukas's eyes popped open, accompanied by a hiss.

This night, Helma was aware, was a pivotal point in her life. She sat in the darkness, floating between Yesterday and Tomorrow. Had she feared this very future, as Ruth once claimed?

A decision had been made, No, she corrected herself, *she* had made the decision, and as always, once Helma Zukas had decided, she stepped forward, eyes clear, certain, and yes: eager.

CHAPTER 23

The Bells Ring

"I'm in charge of getting you to the church on time," Ruth's voice came over the phone at seven in the morning, an unusual hour for Ruth to be awake and a sure sign she hadn't been to bed yet. "I'll be there at nine a.m. sharp."

Helma hung up and sighed. The chances of Ruth showing up at "nine a.m. sharp," were slim to none. She laid a simple blue dress on her freshly made bed, not at all trusting the wedding ensemble would be delivered in time for...she swallowed... in time for the ceremony.

Neither her mother nor Wayne called, and she phoned the hospital for Aunt Em's condition one more time, relieved to hear the noncommittal, "Resting comfortably."

And then she filled her bathtub and soaked for seventeen minutes and after that, took a quick rinse in the shower and carried on, pretending she was preparing for a day at the library. She played Handel's *Water Music* to reinforce the idea of it being just a normal day, keeping a tea cup filled with hot tea, which she periodically emptied into her sink because she forgot to drink it.

At the appointed hour of "nine a.m. sharp," she removed her car keys from her purse, preparing to drive herself to the hospital. But at that exact moment, her doorbell jangled with Ruth's signature ring.

"Let's go," Ruth said when Helma opened the door, already turning to descend the staircase.

"Ruth," Helma said. "You look... beautiful."

Ruth stopped and twirled. "Like it?"

She wore a drapey, deep violet dress with an even deeper violet shawl, black stockings and 4-inch black heels. On anyone else, the outfit might be extreme, on Ruth it was shockingly subdued.

"I do."

Ruth chortled. "Hold that thought until you're in front of the altar."

"Altar?" Helma said, startled. "Is there a priest? A minister? A judge? I forgot to arrange for someone to officiate."

"All taken care of. C'mon. I cleaned my car for this event. Well, I didn't clean it; I paid the sixteen-year-old delinquent next door to do it."

Ruth hummed all the way to the hospital, pausing once to say, "Hey, thanks for the maid-of-honor invite," before she returned to humming what sounded like the theme to "The Addams Family," a favorite show of Helma's brother, Bruce.

And that reminded her. "My brothers! And cousins. Wayne's family. We didn't tell them."

"Plenty of time for that later. We'll have a hell of a big party. Maybe you can skip telling your cousin Ricky for a couple of years, though."

Ruth pulled into the hospital parking lot. Helma started. How had they arrived at the hospital so quickly?

"Oh look," Ruth pointed. "There's Carter,"

"Carter? Why is Carter here?"

Ruth shrugged, but the corners of her mouth tipped upward. "We got to talking last night, you know."

Carter looked up at Ruth's car and a smile lit his face. Helma couldn't recall ever seeing the dour detective smile, not such an unself-conscious, helpless smile. Curious and curiouser.

"Room 322 next to your aunt's room is empty," a dark-haired nurse told Helma as she and Ruth passed the nurses' station. "Your dress has already been delivered, and you can get ready there."

Helma blinked at the swooping silver crepe paper decorating the desk at the nurses' station; and were those cardboard silver bells?

"Want help?" Ruth asked.

"Please."

"Really? Great." Ruth turned to the nurse. "Can you hang a 'keep out' sign on the door? Bad luck to see the bride."

"My mother—" Helma began.

"Especially mothers," Ruth said sternly, and led the way to Room 322.

Ruth fussed and fretted worse than Helma guessed her mother would have, pinning, pulling pins and repinning, adjusting drapes and straps, and sticking an emergency curler in Helma's hair before she attached a veil. A veil? Helma couldn't remember trying on a veil in the Bridal Bar.

Through Room 322's window, she watched a thin strip of sunshine lighten the concrete walls of the south wing of the hospital, barely noting Ruth's, "Stand still. Good girl."

Finally Ruth stepped back and surveyed Helma, grinning.

"Are we finished? Is it time? Can we go now?" Helma turned toward the door, hampered by long skirts and—good heavens— she was shocked to see, a short train.

"Might want to change those shoes." Ruth pointed to a tip of brown loafer peeking clumsily from beneath the white shimmery hem. She pulled a pink shoebox from under a pile of clothes on the hospital bed. "Here they are."

The shoes were white satin and fit perfectly.

"One last thing," Ruth said, opening the hospital room's bathroom door. "Take a look at yourself in the mirror."

Helma stared. She barely recognized herself. "I'm...very...white."

"Bridal," Ruth amended. She glanced at her watch. "Four minutes to lift-off." She smoothed a tuck in the waistline. "Any last words?"

"Thank you, Ruth."

"No problem."

"Is that an accordion?" Helma asked.

"That's our cue." With sweeping ceremony, Ruth opened the door of 322, and beckoned her forward.

Helma was met by a crowd of people lining the corridor. A blur of faces: Walter David without Moggy, Ms. Moon in a sari and her hands held in prayerful attitude, George Melville grinning. Glory Shandy beamed on the arm of Mister Dubois, dressed like a grown-up.

She was vaguely aware of sighs and gasps, thumbs up and a "Yay, Helma" from Harley. The door of 324 opened in front of her. It too was packed with people.

"My baby," Helma heard her mother say, and then immediately burst into sobbing.

"Wilhelmina," Aunt Em breathed.

Positioned to face her, the only face she clearly saw, with his warm eyes and outreaching hand, dressed in a gray tuxedo, was Chief of Police Wayne Gallant.

CHAPTER 24

Chapter the Final

"Your plane's at three, Helma. Let's go," Ruth said. "Carter's got the car running. Don't make him use the siren."

Helma glanced around her apartment. Most of the furniture had already been moved, the refrigerator was empty and blocked open, a box of baking soda inside. Only Boy Cat Zukas remained, and he was crouched in the back of her closet, where he'd retreated the day before when the moving had begun in earnest.

Ruth shook the cat carrier. "Maybe I should have brought a stun gun."

Helma entered her nearly bare bedroom with Ruth behind her. "Let me try one more time," Ruth said, kneeling down and reaching a hand toward the rear corner of the closet.

Quicker than quick, Boy Cat Zukas slashed out at her, hissing.

Ruth jerked backward and landed on her bottom. Three lines of scratches raked the back of her hand, beads of blood popping from them. "Little bastard. Look what he did. I quit. It's up to you."

"We can't leave him here," Helma told her.

"You're right."

"I don't touch cats."

Ruth stood. "Like he's going to let you touch him, the wretched beast."

Helma retrieved a dish towel from her kitchen and laid it on the floor of the entrance to her closet so she wouldn't mar her traveling clothes. She knelt carefully, smoothing the fabric over her knees to avoid wrinkles. Boy Cat Zukas stared at her. He kneaded the carpet with his paws as if preparing for another slash, and maybe a desperate scramble past her out of the closet. She'd already closed the doors so he couldn't leap to the balcony and disappear over the roof of the Bayside Arms.

Helma and the cat contemplated one another. "C'mon, c'mon," Ruth said, tapping her foot. "Time is flinging past."

Helma cleared her throat and tentatively extended her hand toward Boy Cat Zukas. She rarely spoke to animals except to issue commands. "I think he might be frightened," she told Ruth.

"That miscreant? Hah."

"Come out of there," Helma said, trying to inject a conversational tone into her voice.

He stared at her.

"We have to leave now," she tried.

Nothing.

Cautiously, she reached her hand forward, inch by inch into the closet, holding it steady, not even wiggling her fingers. Something damp and cold touched her fingertips. She swallowed, forcing herself not to jerk backward.

Then she felt fur rubbing against her fingers and bent lower to see Boy Cat Zukas pressing his head against her palm. She carefully reached in with her other hand and gripped him behind the shoulders, pulling him unresistingly from the closet, ignoring Ruth's, "I'll be damned."

She hadn't known cats were so soft. Her arms were held out straight, and Boy Cat Zukas hung uncomplainingly from the grip of her hands beneath his armpits.

"Open the carrier door," she told Ruth.

Ruth did, and ever so briefly, Helma held Boy Cat Zukas to her neck, feeling him press fleetingly against her cheek, before nudging him inside. She felt the rumble of purrs against her hands as she pushed him toward the new cat bed she'd bought for the carrier.

"I left directions for his care on the table," she told Ruth.

"Directions? You left me a book."

Helma's mother, her arm through TNT's, waited on the sidewalk, Wayne beside them, as Carter parked in the loading zone in front of the terminal.

"All set?" Wayne asked her, removing her carry-on from Carter's trunk.

"All set," Helma said, glancing one last time into the back seat where Boy Cat Zukas appeared to be contentedly sleeping inside his carrier.

"I didn't think they were going to finish this in time," Lillian said, holding out the urn to Helma. "Did you leave room in your carry-on?"

Helma nodded, opening her new carry-on, and her mother slid the bronze urn inside, pausing to gently pat it, her eyes damp. "Bye, Em," she whispered, then coughed and said to Helma in a husky voice, "The certificate's in this envelope. Don't forget where to do it."

"The Nemunas Valley, near the river."

Lillian nodded. She patted Helma's hair, and, for a horrible moment, Helma expected her mother to lick her finger and dab at a smudge on Helma's cheek. "Now, do you have your tickets, and your passports? Be sure to send us a postcard from Vilnius." She reached for TNT's hand.

"We will. We have to go, Mother."

"Oh, have fun. Just have fun. Goodbye, goodbye. *Viso gero.*"

"Don't forget to bring back the 999," Ruth reminded her one last time. "All three kinds."

As the plane lifted off and circled the airport to begin the first leg of their long journey, Helma squeezed Wayne's hand and gazed down through the oval window. She saw them, four small figures standing near the airport fence, waving. And waving.

Author's Note

I've lived with Miss Helma Zukas for more than fifteen years. During those years, she took up residence in the back of my head, prodding me to pay attention, to take notes, to view through her eyes all the juicy bits she'd like to do or say or comment on—or even change.

In this, her twelfth adventure, the title, *Farewell, Miss Zukas*, is bittersweet. I leave her as she herself departs one phase of her life and steps into another, exciting era—out there somewhere.

Helma Zukas grew from my own experience as a librarian: of eye-rolling over librarian jokes; of watching one of the greatest professions in the world tangle itself up fussing over its image; of seeing brilliant, capable women (and men) feel complimented when someone asserted they didn't act like "real" librarians.

"Real" librarians—the best librarians—share common traits: curiosity, the ability to organize, to spread the excitement of ideas and reading. They are crack researchers and champions of your right to read whatever you desire. They *do* love to read. If they don't know where to find information, they know *how* to find it. And well, yes, they do frequently share curious idiosyncrasies.

I wanted to write a series starring a librarian, but what kind of a librarian? Someone who would bust through the stereotypes?

When I create a character, I sit with my 0.9 mechanical pencil and yellow paper and ask myself questions. "What happened to her when she was eight that no one will ever know?" "What food does she refuse to eat?" I answer my own questions as I go along, building my character. Near the end of my "interview" with Helma Zukas, I asked the question, "Is Helma a virgin?" The answer I jotted down without hesitation, was, "None of your business."

At that moment, I knew Miss Zukas had come to life. She was tough, honest, crafty, a complicated woman with a deep but futile desire to perceive the world in black and white. And yes, she was a "real" librarian. I embraced the stereotype. Helma was unapologetic.

The name Zukas is my favorite aunt's Lithuanian married name. The name Helma comes from Wilhelmina because I wanted a beautiful name to have an unbeautiful nickname. My apologies to any Helmas out there.

I was fortunate to come of age during a brief window of time among a community packed with Lithuanian immigrants—over-emotional, tradition-ridden, raucous, often hard-drinking. The older generation clung to an old-country past while the younger wanted to disappear into the future of America. It was a Push-Me Pull-You time, seasoned by a fervent Catholicism bordering on paganism. It provided a rich tapestry for me to draw from.

So many of us, especially women, have friendships similar to Helma and Ruth's: friends who we would die for, but who, after ninety minutes in their company, begin to drive us nuts. I wanted to honor those rich and sometimes frustrating, but always indestructible bonds.

I'm grateful to the wisdom of Marjorie Braman, my first editor at Avon/Harper, who insisted that Helma and Ruth share the center stage of every mystery, and especially to Lyssa Keusch, also at Avon/Harper, who ushered through the next ten Miss Zukas mysteries, and whose gentle hand always kept me on track.

I confess I've borrowed ideas and quirks from friends and colleagues, and I've delighted in stories and experiences shared by readers—but I've never, as I was once accused, "changed my looks so I could work undercover and steal peoples' personalities."

My eternal gratitude to my dear friend, Margaret. And to Linda, Ruth, Gillian, and Dorothy, and many more, who generously shared library experiences. To Kip, and to Tom, who never wavered. And my children, who came to believe that Miss Zukas was their cousin.

I'm grateful to Jurgita in Lithuania, who shared her beloved country with my sister and me, and who connected us to Danute, who shared Zarasai with us, and took us to visit the magnificent ancient oak tree of Stelmužė.

Mostly, I want to thank the generous and gracious readers who took Helma and Ruth, and even Ms. Moon, into their hearts – and worried over Boy Cat Zukas. You are cherished.

Libraries will always be with us. Formats and missions may change, but we will always love and lust for stories, and honor those who keep them accessible for us.

Sometimes when I'm writing, I'm reminded how solitary writing is, how I am telling you a story, and we are holding a very intimate conversation, you and I. I write alone, you read alone. I love that image. To an author, a library truly is heaven, because we're confident that as long as there are libraries, years after we're gone, the words we write will still exist in one form or another, and we will still be able to hold that intimate conversation with you.

Jo Dereske
February 11, 2011

Made in the USA
Lexington, KY
24 October 2011